THE KINGDOM

Preacher Brothers, 1

JENIKA SNOW

THE KINGDOM (PREACHER BROTHERS, 1)

By Jenika Snow

www.JenikaSnow.com

Jenika_Snow@Yahoo.com

Copyright © December 2019 by Jenika Snow

First ebook publication © December 2019 Jenika Snow

Cover design by: Lori Jackson

Editor: Kasi Alexander

Content Editor: Kayla Robichaux

The Preacher Boys.

That's what they called us.

Four brothers born and raised in the criminal lifestyle... in stealing.

Professional thieves. That's what we were. And we were damn good at it. Take what we wanted with no regrets, no repercussions. We didn't have attachments, no worries, and sure as hell no women to screw up the plan. And that's what made our lives work.

The job was set—should have been an in-and-out situation. Easy.

But then I saw her, Amelia, and she wasn't part of the plan. I instantly wanted her, had to have her. She was like this drug, and I was desperately addicted.

I'd do anything, whatever it took to make her mine.

When her life was in danger, when it was Cullen, my own brother, about to hurt her, there was only one thing I could do.

Take her, keep her with me, and make her see she was meant to be mine.

But to Cullen, she was a liability. He wouldn't stop, not when all he could see was making sure the family was safe, that the Preacher Boys were in the clear.

What he didn't know was, family or not, Amelia was the one thing I'd always wanted, and I wouldn't let anyone take her away from me.

Chapter One

Dom

It was almost as good as sex. Hell, in some instances, it was better than having a tight little piece of ass in my bed.

I was a professional fucking thief. This was what I did for a living. This was what got me hard.

My blood raced, my heart pounded, and adrenaline pumped through my veins.

Despite what we were about to do—lift from this motherfucking jewelry store—my mind was crystal clear. It always was. It had to be. Any error, any small discrepancy in the plan, would mean we'd get pinched. No way were any of us going back to fucking jail.

I focused on the jewelry store across the street and brought the walkie-talkie up to my mouth. "Frankie?" I prompted into the piece of plastic, hearing static before the click of him answering.

"We're all set," he said, and I shoved the walkie into the glovebox.

I turned my attention toward Wilder, who sat in the driver seat. Cullen was with Frankie at the back of the store, making sure things went smoothly on their end. I had my skull mask looped around my neck but reached down and pulled it up, covering the lower half of my face.

I looked at Wilder and watched as he did the same thing. He looked over at me, the white grinning skull jaw on the black material looking a little ominous.

"You ready?" I asked.

He nodded once in response. I focused forward once more, then looked down at my watch. The sun had already set, the lights in the store were off, and foot traffic was nonexistent.

"Owner was the only one left. Should be easy enough to get this done." Wilder's voice was muffled behind the fabric.

We'd been casing the jewelry store over the last week. We knew when they took their lunches, when shift change was. We knew what time the mailman dropped off their fucking letters and when the shipments arrived. And on this Thursday—today—they were due to get a box full of gems and diamonds.

It sure as fuck helped that the truck driver was an old cellmate of Frankie's and had given us the tip. We'd kick him back a few for his troubles, and that would be that.

And then the front lights went off in the store, the owner pulling down the security bars over the window, and that was our cue. Wilder and I got out of the van, one that said Harrison Brothers Dry Cleaning and Services on the side. We wore matching uniforms, the name John stitched on the upper right-hand corner of Wilder's shirt, and Clark stitched on mine.

Once across the street, we pressed our bodies up against the side of the building and looked around, making sure shit was legit and quiet. I looked over at Wilder and he nodded once.

And then we moved to the back, where we could see Cullen and Frankie sitting in the old-as-fuck sedan Cullen stole earlier today. The car was parked between the two buildings, the alley dark, no light penetrating.

Frankie and Cullen sat in the front seat, their

skull masks covering the lower half of their faces, same as us.

The gem and diamond shipment had just been received an hour before. And although the vault the store had was pretty heavy duty, it wasn't anything Wilder—our master locksmith and hacker—couldn't crack.

"Four cameras on the exterior, two in the front, one on the side, and two in the back," I spat as I double-checked my gear.

"Ready, Clark?" Wilder teased as he looked down at my name badge.

I lifted my hand and flipped him off.

Although we didn't specifically need these fake-as-fuck uniforms, portraying something we weren't was half the way to not getting caught. The other half was knowing how to get shit done and get it done right.

Look like you're someone else. Act like you own the world. That's how we succeeded in what we did.

"Let's go," I said, and Cullen and Frankie climbed out of the car, with Frankie going to the trunk and opening it. He grabbed the black duffel and closed the lid silently. The duffel held all the tools Wilder would need for cracking the safe, as well as a few items we'd need to clean up afterward.

Cullen handed out the black beanies and we put them on.

"We'll look like a couple of punk assholes," Cullen said, and we all grunted in approval.

"Better to look like a bunch of punk assholes than be identified and be motherfuckers behind bars," Wilder said in a gruff voice. I tipped my chin toward the building and we all started moving forward. We could bullshit later. Until then, it was time to focus.

Chapter Two

Amelia

I rubbed my eyes, the table lamp in front of me bright and slightly blinding, but it allowed me to see the inventory forms in front of me, the ones that were printed so small I practically needed a damn magnifying glass to read them.

Richard was in the front doing a last-minute sweep of what we needed to order, which was the reason I'd agreed to stay and help. It was the end of the month check, and I always felt so bad he had to do the shit all by himself.

He was old and a widower, having lost his wife five years ago, and I knew this jewelry store was his life. Hell, he and his wife had opened it over twenty years ago, something she'd dreamed about starting, and he hadn't denied her. And it had turned out to be very successful. I kind of thought of him as the father I'd never really had. Not to mention he worked around my school schedule.

I felt a twinge of guilt at that last thought.

A shitty childhood, an abusive father, and a mother who was looking for love in all the wrong places and had ignored me on most occasions. But I'd adapted, grown into the person I was today. And that's what mattered. Then Richard had given me a job, a young girl with no work history, who'd come in to the interview with a ripped blouse and stained slacks. He hired me and over the years had become someone I trusted and cared about.

But what would Richard think or say if he knew I actually wasn't even going to school anymore, that I didn't register for classes because my financial aid had fallen through and I just couldn't afford it?

Would he be disappointed? Would he consider me a liar, a failure?

Or maybe he'd understand that life happened, that I had to eat and pay my rent, and there was always next fall, or even summer classes.

I closed my eyes and rested my head in my hands, so exhausted that all these numbers were starting to blend together. Technically, I wasn't even licensed to be doing this stuff, but Richard trusted me. He knew I'd never screw him over.

I heard something out the back door but didn't pay much attention to it. With the tattoo shop right next door, and the bar directly behind us, there was usually commotion in the ally in the form of drunken people or friends loitering. But it being a Thursday night and rather late meant those other two businesses were closed.

I leaned back in my chair and stared at the paperwork, grabbing a pen and marking inventory. The sooner I got this done, the sooner I could go home, maybe take a long, hot bubble bath, drink a glass of wine… or three.

Another five minutes passed, when I heard a thump at the front of the store. Being in the back office meant I was kind of secluded, with the door shut and a row of filing cabinets blocking my view. I listened, not hearing anything and about to go back to work, when I heard a very muffled, deep grunt.

I stood, feeling my brows knit as I stared at the door, which I could now see over the row of stainless steel gray filing cabinets. "Richard?" I called out his name and waited a second, not hearing him and growing a little bit concerned. He was old, so maybe he'd fallen, hit his head on a display case?

I took a step forward, but before I could reach the back door, there was a buzzing sound behind me. I looked over my shoulder just as it was thrown open, two very big men storming inside dressed in what appeared to be some kind of dry cleaning uniform. But it was clear they were here for a very different reason, if their skull masks were anything to go by.

For a moment, I was frozen, unable to move or think or speak. I heard more commotion coming from the front of the store, but I couldn't even think or react. And as one of the men came closer, it was finally as if an electrical charge shot through my body and I snapped into action.

Both men stared at me, the one closest to me moving an inch closer. I stared into his blue eyes, his dark eyebrows visible and a sharp contrast to the crisp color of his irises.

My survival instincts coursed through me. I darted for the front of the store—my only exit, since they were still blocking the rear entrance. But before I could reach out and grip the handle, one of the men grabbed my upper arm. His touch was like fire, singeing me, seeping into my bloodstream. It wasn't painful, but I couldn't deny how it made me feel or explain why I felt it so pronounced.

I gasped out on instinct and looked over my shoulder to see Blue Eyes staring down at me. "Easy," he said softly. God, he was big and muscular, making me feel like a tiny speck in his world. "I thought you said it was only the one asshole?" The man with the blue eyes was the one to speak, his focus never leaving me.

"Yeah, I thought so too," the other man answered, his gaze dark and dangerous, his eyes like spilled ink. Like the very devil himself. This man terrified me and I had no idea why. His voice was deep and serrated, cruel and violent.

"It was only supposed to be that one motherfucker," Blue Eyes said again, and I swallowed in fear as I pressed my back to the wall, his hand no longer wrapped around me.

The commotion in the front of the store was getting louder, seemingly more violent. I felt my eyes widen, tears tracking down my cheeks. The one with the dark eyes loomed over me; the only thing I could see on his face was his eyes, dark and lifeless as he looked at me. And those masks, those skeleton masks that were so damn terrifying, reminded me of death.

"D, wanna go check on them?" he said to Blue Eyes.

For a second, the one named D didn't move, and I snapped my focus to him. He stood only a few feet from us, looking down at me, his eyes locked on mine.

"Dude, you going or you want me to?"

Blue Eyes looked at the other man then back at me. "Don't touch her," he said, and I looked at the scary man to see his brows knitted.

"What the fuck?"

But Blue Eyes gave me a look before turning, as if he was forcing himself to leave. I heard the door to the front of the store open. There was muffled conversation and deep voices. I heard Richard grunting in pain and felt my tears come harder and faster. I had to do something, anything.

The man with the dark eyes looked over his shoulder, and I snapped my gaze to my desk, to where my cell phone lay.

I jerked my head back in his direction just as he turned around to face me once more, his eyes narrowing. Was he smart enough, in tune enough with his surroundings, to know what I was thinking?

I had a feeling that told me yeah, he probably was.

Chapter Three

Amelia

"P-Please...." I'm not sure what I was begging for. My safety? My life? I assumed these men had no intention of killing us or they wouldn't have their faces covered. But I didn't know how the mind of a criminal worked. Maybe even desperate ones at that.

And then a sliver of anger crept up that I'd resorted to begging in the first place.

I slowly stood straighter, the wall to my back, my hands flat against it. I kept my focus right on him, my eyes locked on his. Fuck him—all of them —for making me feel this way. If he thought I was going to be their victim, if they thought I'd let them terrorize me... they were sadly mistaken.

I lived with an abusive father, an absentee mother.

He was nothing to me.

He couldn't do to me anything that hadn't already been done.

And then I saw the corners of his eyes crinkle as if he were grinning, maybe knowing my thoughts.

"You gonna play by the rules, Red?"

I narrowed my eyes at his little nickname, presumably because of my red hair.

"Yeah, that's what I thought. You got fire in you." His gaze dropped to my waist and I felt a chill move through me. "Wonder if you're a natural redhead."

"Fuck you," I spat out and clenched my teeth.

Even with the mask on, I knew that pissed him off. Maybe my words weren't what he was used to hearing, not something he was used to being directed at him.

I didn't know these men, these criminals, thieves, but I had no doubt they were used to getting what they wanted. Hell, they took what wasn't theirs. The sense of entitlement in these pricks pissed me off.

We were at this standstill, staring at each other, the sound of glass breaking coming from the front of the store. I had to do something. I wasn't a hero, not by any means, but when I heard Richard grunt in pain again, something in me snapped. I wasn't going to let the only person who gave a shit about me get hurt, not when I could try to stop it.

I might fail, but doing nothing wasn't trying. It was submitting, letting another asshole try to walk all over me.

The masked asshole looked over his shoulder, his body partially turned. "What the fuck is going on out there? You guys are making so much noise."

I edged toward the desk, only a foot or so from me, reached out for my phone, and quickly moved back to where I had just been at the same time he turned to face me once more. I had my phone pressed to the back of my thigh, feeling my heart race, feeling like he knew what I'd done, that I was "guilty." But he said nothing, just watched me.

More glass breaking had the masked prick cursing. "What in the fuck?" He looked over his shoulder again. "One of you come in here and babysit, and I'll go out there and get this shit done quietly."

I glanced down at my phone and started dialing.

Nine.

One.

One.

Before I could hit Enter, the phone was ripped from my hand and I gasped in shock.

Something in me came alive and I lunged at him, knowing I had no chance. He was big, muscular. I was blinded by fear and anger, not just for myself but for Richard as well. Was he even alive?

I reached up, my fingers curling around the material of his mask, and before I knew what was happening, I pulled it off. For a second time, I stood still as I stared up at him. His short dark hair was mussed, the pure rage on his face clear and tangible.

"You fucking bitch. Now I have to put a bullet in that pretty head of yours." He reached behind him and produced a gun, cocking it and lifting it until it was pointed at me.

I moved back, the tears slipping down my cheeks again, my arms raised and my hands outstretched, palms facing him.

"No. No, no, no." I said that word over and over again like a broken record.

Everything stood still. Time. My life. The situation. And despite me begging, despite how I probably looked scared as hell, I didn't feel anything. I was this void, no emotion, no feelings. Nothing.

I stared at his darkened eyes, feeling myself sober up, knowing this wasn't the end. It was the beginning of whatever was next.

I lowered my arms and looked right in his eyes. "Fuck. You." I sneered those words. "I'm not afraid of you." For a second, I swore his eyes widened in shock, but then that mask was figuratively put back in place.

He took a step toward me, and then another and another until he was right in front of me. He lifted his arm higher, and I felt the coldness of the gun pressed right to my forehead.

He leaned in an inch. "How about now? Fuck me now, Red?"

Before I could answer, could say anything, the gun was ripped from my forehead, the man with the dark eyes grunting as his body was hauled away from me, his form slamming against the wall beside me. I gasped and covered my mouth with my hands, feeling my eyes widen even farther.

The sight before me was filled with silence, even

more so than any event that had happened in the last few moments of them breaking in.

Blue Eyes had the other man against the wall, his thickly muscled forearm pressed to the unmasked man's face.

"What the fuck, D?" the man pressed to the wall grated out, his voice thick as if he couldn't get enough air into his lungs.

"I told you not to touch her." The sound of D's voice was muffled behind the mask, but I could hear the venom in it, the anger… red-hot rage.

Both men stared at each other, saying nothing for several long moments, the tension in the air thick.

"She's seen my face, D. She's seen my fucking face."

D looked over at me, his blue eyes so vibrant in this moment, as if his anger made the color even more intense. I couldn't move, couldn't even breathe.

"I told you not to fucking touch her," he said and slowly looked back at the other man.

"What the fuck, D? What the actual fuck?"

D stepped back, dropping his arm from the other man's throat. "You plan on what, fucking killing her?"

The other man stayed silent, but I saw the answer on his face.

Yeah, he had every intention of pulling that trigger.

"You touch her, fucking look at her, Cullen, and fucking things won't be good for you." D hissed out the words.

"Now you're fucking saying my name in front of her?" Cullen leaned in, his lip curled in a snarl. "What the fuck is up with you tonight with this bitch?"

It looked like Blue Eyes was about to say something, the anger shooting out of him like a cold front, but the sound of footsteps approaching had the room stilling.

"Damn, is the pissing contest over with, so we can get the hell out of here?"

I snapped my head in the direction of the front of the store, where two more men wearing matching skull masks stood in the doorway, their gazes darting between D and Cullen before landing on me.

"We need to get the fuck out of here," Cullen said and pushed D away from him. He glanced and me and snarled. "Do whatever the fuck you want with her, but if we get pinched because of this, you're the one going down, brother." Cullen kept his focus on me the whole time. "And so will she."

A low growl filled the room, like a wild animal had been set free. I realized it came from Blue Eyes.

"Let's get the fuck out of here," one of the masked men said, standing by the door that led to the front of the store.

Before I knew what was happening, Blue Eyes had his hand wrapped around my upper arm and was hauling me out the back door, the other men following, Cullen staring at me with so much hatred I felt it.

I looked over my shoulder into the front of the store and could see Richard slowly standing, a smear of blood on his cheek. A sigh of relief left me, this weight off my shoulders. He was alive. Thank God.

I didn't know what Blue Eyes had planned for me, but I knew one thing for certain. I had to survive. There was no other option.

Chapter Four

Dom

I knew she was aware I hadn't taken my focus off her since we got in the back of the van. She'd kept glancing over at me, shadows and a yellow glow playing across her face from the intermittent streetlights we passed.

I'd taken off my mask, but Wilder kept his on, clearly still on edge with this whole situation. I didn't blame them, couldn't blame any of my brothers for how they reacted. I would have been the same way. But they needed to understand this was what I wanted and I wouldn't be swayed.

Not one fucking bit.

Our place was a good half an hour from the

jewelry store, a home that had been our father's before he passed away. He'd been a bastard to us while growing up, a drug dealer and drug-addicted criminal who had taught us all we knew.

I guess we owed him something for that.

But the prick died and hadn't left us anything. Not a cent. Not even the house we lived in. Once everything had been settled, we bought the fucking thing. We could have just left, gotten a new home, but for all the shit and bad memories that had gone down in that place, we'd also had a lot of good ones.

We built onto it, extended the rooms, finished the basement so we all would have our own living quarters, separate homes within one main structure.

And it worked out pretty fucking nicely too.

"I don't know what the fuck you think you're going to do with her, but we need to have a meeting when we get back," Wilder said, and I glanced over at him, seeing his eyes in the rearview mirror a second before he looked back at the road.

We ditched the dry-cleaning van and were now in some piece of shit perv-mobile. Well, that's what Wilder called it, one of those sketchy vans that would've been featured in some after-school special about not taking candy from the back of strangers' vehicles.

I didn't respond, just turned my focus back to her. Hell, I practically smelled her fear. It was tangible, and I wouldn't lie and say the knowledge that she was afraid but pretended to be strong didn't turn me on.

It gave me a power high.

The rest of the trip was done in silence, and I kept my focus on her the entire fucking time. I couldn't help it, couldn't stop myself. I couldn't even explain what it was about her that made me feel this way, that made me feel crazed and possessive enough I would attack my brother, stake my claim right there on a fucking job.

I was crazed enough that, for the first time in my life, I wasn't solely focused on the job at hand; I was acting totally out of character. I took a hostage... fucking kidnapped her, because of one reason.

I wanted her.

Wilder slowed, and I knew we were coming up to the house we all once grew up. But once we'd grown up, Frankie and Wilder had moved out right after Cullen had. They'd wanted me to sell the house, but maybe it was sentiment, or hell, investment that had made me keep it. Although we'd had shitty memories with our father growing up here, I also had some pretty incredible ones with my brothers.

I knew the rest of my brothers were in another van behind us, and I knew I'd get a hell of a lot of shit for bringing her back here, more than I'd gotten from Cullen back at the jewelry store.

"Blindfold her," Wilder said, and it wasn't a question. It was a demand.

I snapped my attention to him and growled low, wanting to head in his direction, to put him in his fucking place. But I knew he was right. Although I had no intention of letting her go, she didn't need to see any more than I had already shown her.

I wasn't just talking about the drive up here either. She'd seen a side of me not even my brothers had seen. And that was dangerous. She made me even more dangerous and unstable.

There was a scrap of material on the floor of the van and I picked it up, moving closer to her. She stiffened and pressed her back against the van, her eyes wide. I smelled her fear like I was some kind of animal, this potent aroma that had every protective instinct in me rising. It also turned me on.

I wanted to tell her not to be worried, that I

wouldn't let anything hurt her. But instead, I kept my mouth shut, narrowed my eyes, and put that hard, cold exterior in place. I couldn't let anyone know she made me weak, made me feel these things. I'd already shown more emotion than I ever had in my fucking life, and I didn't even know who she was, didn't know her name, how old she was… didn't fucking know a goddamn thing about her.

All I knew was that for the first time in my life, since that first moment I saw her, I wanted her like no other. I'd do anything to have her. And that meant attacking my brother on the job.

"It's for your own protection. It's for the best," I said gruffly, our eyes locked. A second passed, but then I saw the moment she gave in, submitted. It wasn't like she had a choice.

I wrapped the strip of material around her eyes, and I don't even try to hide the fact that I let the silky strands of her dark-red hair play across my fingers. I also didn't fucking stop myself from leaning in an inch and closing my eyes as I inhaled deeply, taking in the floral scent that clung to the strands.

She stiffened. "What are you doing?" she asked softly, so low only I heard. I didn't move, my face so close, my mouth a couple inches from hers.

Fuck, I wanted to kiss her. Instead, I finished tying the material and pulled back, clearing my throat and glancing at Wilder. He watched me from the rearview mirror again, his brows pulled low. I knew he'd seen the interaction, but I didn't fucking care.

I didn't care about anything or anyone in this moment but her.

Chapter Five

Amelia

I felt the vehicle stop, heard car doors opening and closing. Then there was silence except for my frantic breathing. He'd blindfolded me. That had to be a good sign, right? That had to mean he wouldn't kill me? Surely if he kept me in the literal dark, where I couldn't identify anything, that was a good sign, right?

Or maybe I was just hoping for too much. Maybe I was praying this wouldn't end up with me being buried in an unmarked grave out in the middle of nowhere.

Although he'd placed the material over my eyes, I remembered what he looked like without the mask. His image would forever be ingrained in my mind.

His features were masculine, his jaw square, his lips full. His nose was straight but not harsh. The dark slashes of his eyebrows accented his bright blue eyes. God, he was just as beautiful as he was dangerous.

The sound of the back door to the van opening pulled me out of my thoughts, and my entire body went ramrod straight. I felt lightheaded as I breathed hard and fast, terrified, nervous, feeling like I'd most definitely pass out if I stood.

"Breathe," I heard him say close to me in his deeply masculine voice. For some reason, it calmed me.

I expected him to be rough as he pulled me out of the van, but his hands were gentle on me, soothing almost.

I didn't like that, didn't like how my body reacted to him.

I was stumbling around even though he held on to me, the sound of my breathing filling my ears. I felt like I'd passed out, but he kept me close to his big body, the hardness of his chest and arms making me feel extremely small and vulnerable, very feminine.

I heard several sets of doors opening, and although I couldn't see in front of me, when I looked down, beneath the blindfold, there was a sliver of an opening, a minute area that wasn't obscured. I could see a hardwood floor, my shoes soft on it as I was pulled forward. More doors opened and closed, and then we stopped for a second. I heard them talking, these deep murmurs that were far too low for me to understand what was being said, but still he kept his arm on me, kept me close.

Whatever they were talking about was heated, their murmurs getting faster, harsher. And then another door opened and it drowned out the conversation.

"We're going to go down some stairs. I won't let you fall."

I didn't know why I believed a word he spoke, but when he said that, I knew it was the truth. He wouldn't let me fall.

I reached out on instinct, my hand landing on smooth drywall as we descended. I could tell the stairs were carpeted, soft and almost plush beneath my shoes. It smelled clean, a mixture of lemon and cotton.

The door we had just come from closed above

us, sounding so far away, as if I'd descended into hell.

Maybe I had.

"One more door, and then we'll be alone," he said huskily, and then I found myself standing alone, his body away from mine, the chill in the air having nothing to do with the actual temperature, but because he wasn't near me anymore.

I wrapped my arms around my waist, I supposed to make myself seem smaller, less noticeable. I was terrified, my heart racing and my palms sweaty. I was still breathing frantically, on the verge of hyperventilating. I had no idea what he had planned for me, but in the back of my mind, I kept telling myself he wouldn't kill me, that he wouldn't go through all this trouble if he just planned on snuffing my life out.

"I'm not sure what you want from me. But I don't have anything. I don't have money or anyone who cares that I'm gone. No one will give you a ransom for me." I was rambling, so scared at this point I was begging, hoping he would sympathize, empathize with me.

He didn't answer, but I could hear him moving around. He wasn't very far away, his presence like this heavy weight surrounding me.

My hands started shaking, but I clenched them tighter around me. "What do you want? What do you plan on doing with me… to me?" I turned my head when I heard him to my left, then did the same when he moved to my right. "Are you going to kill me?" God, my voice was just as shaky as my hands had been.

"No. I'm not going to hurt you," he finally said, and I exhaled in relief, although I didn't know why I believed a word he said.

"I'm no one. I have nothing to offer, nothing you could possibly want." Before I knew what was happening, the blindfold was taken from me, his fingers skimming along the side of my cheek, sending chills along my body.

I blinked, my vision starting to clear, that blurriness waning. The light was harsh, but then it mellowed out, evening in tone.

I held in my gasp when I saw him standing right in front of me. He didn't move, didn't even breathe as he looked at me. I had to crane my neck to look into his face. He blocked out everything behind him, making me feel even smaller than I was in his presence.

"What's your name?"

The way he asked me that I could tell it wasn't a

question but more so a demand. I thought about lying, maybe ignoring him. But in the end, I was truthful. "Amelia." Did he hear me? I'd whispered that and wasn't even sure I said it out loud.

"Amelia."

God, the way it sounded on his lips…

"I'm Dom."

Dom. D. Blue Eyes.

I didn't say his name out loud, didn't want to give him the satisfaction, didn't want to give *me* the satisfaction.

"What do you want?" I asked again, but I was afraid of how he'd respond.

"You know what I want," he said without apology, as if I really did know what he wanted.

"N-no, I have no idea why I'm here, what you want with me." I smoothed my hands down my skirt, a cold sweat covering my entire body.

He didn't move, didn't speak. Then he took a step back, as if he knew I needed the space, needed more air.

And I did.

I sucked in a lungful, trying to calm myself.

"I only want one thing. It's why I brought you here, why I risked everything." I watched in shock as he brought the blindfold to his nose and inhaled, all the while keeping his focus trained right on me.

"W-what?" Although I knew what he was about to say by the way he looked at me.

"You. I want you, Amelia."

Chapter Six

Dom

I didn't want to leave her, but I had to go handle this with my brothers. I knew they'd want to talk about it now. They were probably standing around waiting for me.

I took the steps two at a time, and once I was at the top, I closed the basement door and stood there for a minute, hearing the clock on the wall ticking down the seconds. I didn't waste any time as I headed straight to the garage, knowing that's where they'd be.

I made my way through the living room, into the kitchen, and grabbed the handle to the door that led to the garage. Once opened, I immediately saw my three brothers standing around. The garage was large, spacious, with two cars inside as well as a workout station across from them.

Wilder and Frankie were leaning against Frankie's Corvette, their arms crossed over their chests as they talked softly. Being identical twins made it nearly impossible for others to tell them apart. But for me is was easy, as if there were no doubt in my mind on who was who.

They hadn't even noticed I'd come in. Cullen, on the other hand… his focus was right on me, his gaze hard, his eyes dark and penetrating. He'd give me the most shit. I was pretty confident Frankie and Wilder would fall in line, but Cullen… Cullen was a breed all his own.

"Let's get this shit done and over with," I said, and Frankie and Wilder looked up at me, their conversation instantly ceasing. Nothing was said for long moments, but then Wilder cleared his throat and looked between Frankie and Cullen before his gaze landed back on mine.

"I think I can speak for all of us when I ask—what the fuck are you thinking, and what the hell do you plan on doing with her?"

There were a couple steps leading down from where the garage door was, and I took them, staring my brothers in their eyes and letting each one know this conversation was only going to go one way.

Mine.

"I'm going to do with her whatever the fuck I want to do," I said unapologetically and stared Wilder right in the eyes. Then I did the same to Frankie, and then finally to Cullen.

"You risked a lot of shit, Dom. And for what? A piece of snatch?" Frankie asked, his anger and frustration coming out in his voice.

I growled low and snapped my head in his direction. "You'll do best to watch your fucking mouth."

"So now you're fucking going up against us all, because of some damn female?" Cullen's voice was low, hard, and cold. He was pissed, and I couldn't blame him. I had risked all of us by getting involved with her and bringing her back here.

"I don't expect any of you to understand, but I am expecting you to trust me." I looked each of them in the eyes once more. "As the oldest, I've never steered you wrong. I've never put you in jeopardy—"

"Until tonight," Cullen said calmly but with menace. "Until you fucking kidnapped her... fucking brought her back to our home." Cullen took a step toward me and narrowed his eyes. "You should've let me finish her off right then and there. She can ID me, and now she can identify you, since you were the genius who decided to take off your mask as well. You should've let me fucking put a bullet in her head."

I felt possessiveness, protectiveness over her fill every single part of my body. I stalked toward Cullen until we were nose-to-nose. "We don't kill people, Cullen. We aren't fucking murderers." My anger was rising at the very thought of her being hurt. "I'm not asking. I'm telling you that she's staying here. With me. You don't like it..." I took a step back and eyed Cullen up and down before looking at my other two brothers and doing the same. "If none of you like it, you can get the fuck out of here."

There was a long-ass silence, no one speaking or moving. Hell, I didn't even think anyone breathed. Finally, Frankie cleared his throat, and Wilder lifted his hand to rub his palm over the back of his head.

Neither one of them would look me in the face.

"You know what?" Cullen finally spoke up and shoved his hands in the front pocket of his jeans. "Fuck it. This is your mess, Dom. You deal with it however the fuck you want. I'm out." He looked at

Wilder and Frankie then. "You guys are a bunch of pussies for keeping your mouths shut."

Although they hadn't actually kept their mouths shut, I knew what Cullen was referring to. They hadn't put up much of a fight. Then again, they weren't like Cullen. No one really was.

"Just be in the office to talk about the job in an hour. I'm ready to get this shit squared away and go to bed," Cullen spat before walking out of the garage and back inside.

I knew he'd be the one to give me the biggest issue. He was hardheaded and had emotional problems… meaning he had none. He was as cold, hard, and unmovable as the granite in the kitchen.

But there wouldn't be anything I didn't do to protect her, even if that meant going against my brother.

Chapter Seven

Amelia

He'd left me five minutes ago. He'd shown me to this bedroom and then said he'd be back, leaving me here to wonder what in the hell I was going to do. And here I was right now, sitting on the edge of the massive bed, my hands in my lap, my breathing still frantic.

I knew instantly this room was his, with its darkly colored accents but very minimalistic decor, as if he couldn't be bothered with items adorning the place he lived. Or maybe he just didn't care.

The latter seemed more accurate.

I closed my eyes and rested my head in my

hands, breathing out roughly and trying to think of what I was going to do. What could I do?

I had to breathe, had to control myself, to figure out if I could actually survive this, come out in one piece.

I stood and walked around, looking at the room, running my fingers along everything. There was a small half-bath attached to the room, white subway tiles on the wall and floor, everything looking so barren and clean, crisp and… empty.

There were no windows in the room, because I knew we were in the basement, and it felt kind of like the room was closing in on me, like I was in a box with no air holes.

There was another door opposite the bed, the chrome handle cold in my grasp as I turned it. A closet. Hanging up were black button-down shirts, white tees, and distressed jeans. There were a few black slacks, and I found myself running my fingers over the material.

What the fuck was wrong with me? I needed to figure out how to get out of here.

I closed the door, contemplating tossing his clothes out, destroying the room just for shock value, to be childish—but it wouldn't matter. I didn't want to piss him off.

I stared at the bedroom door, assuming—no, knowing it was locked. He wasn't a stupid man. I knew that, even though I didn't know him. So I found myself sitting on the edge of the bed again and rubbing my eyes. God, I was tired.

The bed was big, but not so massive it took up too much space in the room. And the sheets were dark, soft. Almost like this contrast. Like he was. Dom.

I played his name over and over in my head.

Was it short for something else? Dominik maybe? Why did I even care?

I also didn't like the way it made me feel, how I felt this tingle up my spine when I thought about him or just his name.

And then I thought about the man named Cullen, about how cold and hard he seemed, how lifeless his dark eyes were as he'd stared at me. He would've killed me, taken my life as easily as swatting a fly. He was the one I should've been worried about, not Dom, who saved my life, even though he and the others had put me in danger in the first place.

He was the reason I wasn't on the floor and lifeless, a bullet hole between my eyes, blood pooled around my body.

I pushed those thoughts away and stared at that bedroom door again. Maybe if I pulled on it hard enough, it would open and I'd be able to escape, rip myself from this reality. I stood, about to walk over to do just that, to try my hardest, even though it wasn't like I could actually get out of here. If I was in the basement—which I assumed, because we descended stairs—I'd have to go through several more sets of doors.

These men were thieves, professional ones at that, given how they robbed the jewelry store. They had contingencies in place, probably security cameras, weapons… rough firepower to protect what was theirs.

Hell, they had a gate around the property. That's about the most I'd seen as we pulled up, right before they put the blindfold over my eyes. I took a step toward the door, but right above me I heard pounding, maybe footsteps? Or maybe it was music? Either way, it had me freezing in place, my head cocked back, my focus on the ceiling.

My heart was racing once again as I continued to hear that noise above me. I took a step back toward the bed, and another, until I felt the mattress hit the back of my knees. And then I let myself fall back, sitting down, reaching out and gripping the soft comforter beneath me.

I let my back fall onto the mattress and I stared at the stark-white ceiling. The music was loud but muffled, heavy with bass. I rolled onto my side, got into the fetal position, bringing my knees to my chest, and curled my arms around my legs.

I stared at the wall, at that blank slate, thinking about my life, at the events that had transpired. And for the first time since standing in that jewelry store, I cried.

I cried for Richard and that he was hurt, that his store had been robbed.

I cried for the fact that I couldn't help him, hadn't been able to protect him.

I sobbed when I thought about where my life was headed now, that I had no idea what the future held.

But I cried the hardest, feeling the tears slide down my cheeks and soak the comforter beneath me, because the things I felt for the man who kidnapped me weren't normal… but I felt like they were.

I felt like it's what I'd been missing my whole life.

Chapter Eight

Dom

I heard Cullen slam the door to one of the rooms and turn on some music, the bass pounding through the walls. Although Cullen rarely stayed at the house overnight, I did realize how much time he spent here when all four of us were under the same roof. A part of me assumed it was him wanting to be close—still protecting us even though he didn't need to—and even if he'd never actually admit it. Frankie and Wilder had their own places, as well, but after every job we did together the two of them would stay the night and get piss ass drunk and high. It was almost like a ritual to them at this point.

And here I was, my room, my living quarters in the basement. It was another form of me getting away from everyone and everything. I preferred my solitude, as did my brothers, but instead of selling this fucking house, or even getting my own place like they had, I hung onto it and made it my own, even with all the fucking bad memories attached to it.

I thought of *her*. She was downstairs, waiting for me in my room… because I'd kidnapped her and she was my prisoner.

I heard Frankie and Wilder come inside from the garage, looked over my shoulder and saw they refused to make eye contact. They knew better. They were the youngest out of the four of us and fell in line pretty easily where Cullen and I were concerned. That wasn't to say they didn't have their own mean streaks, their own stubborn natures.

They were Preacher boys, after all.

The twins weren't hardened like Cullen and me. They'd been shielded from our father's anger and annoyance at having to take care of four kids on his own. We were more like workers to our father, little thieves he could mold for his own gain.

Cullen and I had nurtured them the best we could, the best two young boys knew how to. With no mother—well, no mother they remembered—and a slew of random women coming and going for our father's pleasure, we were left to fend for ourselves.

I scrubbed a hand over the back of my head and watched them disappear down the hall toward Frankie's section of the house. No doubt he had a few bottles of whiskey in his room and a stack of joints. It was their routine after a job, their ritual. They'd toss back some shots and smoke a joint before finding out how much we each would get.

Fuck, what was I doing? What was I going to do with Amelia?

I headed back downstairs and stopped when I was right in front of my closed bedroom door. For a second, I contemplated just leaving her be until I could get my thoughts together, but fuck, I wanted to go in there and see her, talk to her, touch her… just fucking look at her.

What has she done to me?

If I believed in witches and paranormal shit, I might have thought she'd cast a spell on me, made me this obsessed maniac who was totally okay with kidnapping a woman and keeping her prisoner in my room.

I listened, but didn't hear anything. I could envision her destroying my room, breaking shit, tossing things against the wall. I certainly couldn't and wouldn't blame her.

I gripped the handle and turned it slowly. The light was still on, the room immaculate… exactly how I'd left it.

That surprised me.

She had control, self-restraint.

I stepped inside. She was curled up in the center of the bed, her shoes still on, her dark-red hair fanned over the blanket. I could see her chest rising and falling softly. She was asleep. I didn't know whether to be pleased by that fact, that she was comfortable enough, felt non-threatened enough to rest, or be pissed and possessive, angry she wasn't more cautious of her surroundings.

All I thought about was how someone as vulnerable and fragile as her was at the mercy of someone stronger and dangerous.

Someone like me.

But I wouldn't hurt her. I'd never hurt her. In fact, I wanted to do the opposite. I wanted to protect her, but maybe I should've protected her from me?

I stepped in farther until I was at the edge of the bed, staring down at her. She looked so small

and innocent, her body tiny but her curves feminine, womanly. I found myself reaching out and
letting my fingers play across the strands of her hair
that lay against the dark comforter. They were soft
like silk. I knew they smelled fucking incredible too.

I remembered the scent from when I was in the
van, sweet and floral, lemony. My cock thickened,
jerking behind the fly of my jeans. I reached out
and adjusted myself, my balls aching as they were
drawn up, my cock getting harder by the second.

I let go of her hair and looked at her face. Her
skin was alabaster, creamy, her lashes a dark-auburn
color, like little crescent shapes across her cheek.
Her eyes were a vibrant green, and although I
couldn't see them at the moment, I remembered
them vividly from when I stared her at the jewelry
store, when they'd been wide and fearful.

She had a lock of hair fallen across her forehead, and I reached out and moved it, letting my
fingers trail along her temple. God, her skin was soft
and smooth. Perfect.

She stirred slightly but otherwise stayed asleep.
The truth was, I could've stood there and stared at
her all night, knowing she was safe even from men
like me. Especially from men like me.

But then I thought about Cullen who was just

upstairs; in fact, the room he was currently holed up in directly above mine. I could hear the steady beat of bass from the music he listened to. I knew he'd be trouble, that he wouldn't let this end, not easily. And I didn't know how to make him see that she was mine, that if he hurt her, things would get drastic. I'd be drastic.

I took a step back and ran my hand over my jaw, the stubble covering my cheeks and chin scratchy.

I forced myself to leave her and went upstairs well before the hour mark when I was supposed to meet everyone to go over the job. Instead, I made a beeline right to where I knew Frankie and Wilder were. Some shots would do me some good, maybe a couple hits off a joint too. Anything would help me at this point, what with my raging arousal and the confusion I felt about what the fuck I was doing with Amelia.

I knocked once before opening the door. A cloud of smoke wafted over my face. It was sweet and potent. The good kind of shit.

I stepped inside and closed the door behind me, needing to numb away some of how I felt. Because if I didn't, there was no way I could control myself or my desire where Amelia was concerned.

Was she worth it, worth the risk? I knew the answer already.

She was. She so fucking was.

Chapter Nine

Dom

"Thirty fucking grand each," Frankie said, and Wilder whistled under his breath.

"Not bad, even with the drama," Wilder said and looked over at me.

I didn't say anything in response as I stood across from them with my back against the wall and my arms crossed over my chest. I felt Cullen staring at me and glanced at him.

"You just as high and drunk as those two assholes?"

I lifted my hand and ran it over my jaw, not answering. He was right, but I wasn't going to bother responding.

Cullen smirked. "I'll have Scarlett work on pushing the jewels to buyers this week. You know the drill." Cullen grabbed a joint and placed it between his lips. "Once that's done, Scarlett will contact me and we'll all get paid." His words were slightly muffled by the joint in his mouth. Cullen lit the end of it and inhaled deeply. He kept the smoke in his lungs for a moment before slowly blowing it out. A cloud of smoke filled the space around him before dissipating.

"Once we get the money, I'll start filtering it through our three properties and cleaning it." Although the guys knew the process, how we laundered the money, how it was all set up so we didn't get caught, I felt the need to reiterate that fact to Frankie and Wilder after every job.

"We know the drill, dude," Frankie said.

"We've been doing this a long time," Wilder replied and grinned, his eyes bloodshot from being high as fuck.

They were smart, damn smart, but they could also be reckless. I supposed that was the benefit of being young and having two older brothers that shouldered most shit.

They lived in the moment, not really thinking about what would happen next. And although that was risky, although it was dangerous, it was also what made them damn good thieves. It's what made all of us damn good thieves.

"Frankie, Wilder?" I waited until they looked up at me before I continued. "Keep your head down and focus on your own shit. No talking about the job when you're at the bar getting drunk."

Both of them scoffed and looked offended, and although I trusted them with my fucking life, had to, I also had this paternal relationship with them.

They nodded and pushed away from the wall. "We done here?" Frankie asked.

I grunted and tipped my head toward the door, watching him and Wilder leave.

"Let's hit up the bar and see about finding some company for tonight," Wilder said to Frankie, his voice distant as they walked away from us.

Then it was just Cullen and me.

I faced him and saw he already watched me, his arms crossed over his chest as he stood there and leaned against the wall. Thick seconds passed, and I knew he was waiting for me to say something, maybe to back down when it came to Amelia.

I wouldn't.

"I don't know if you're so hard up for a piece of

ass that you're not thinking clearly, but I'm giving you the benefit of the doubt." He let those words hang between us for long moments.

I didn't bother responding. It wouldn't have made a difference anyway. Cullen's mind was made up. Besides, I wasn't going to explain myself to him. Cullen had done a lot of shit in his life—deplorable shit—throughout the years. But it had been for us. It was always for us and our protection as far as Cullen was concerned.

And I might have given him shit about it each and every time, but if the roles were reversed, I would have been supportive of what he wanted.

"Put yourself in my shoes, Cullen. How would you feel if you wanted someone so fucking desperately you risked everything to make her yours?" I took a step closer to him. "What if one of us wanted to get rid of her?"

Cullen narrowed his eyes and pushed away from the wall. He didn't speak for a long moment but then exhaled, as if he were frustrated with the situation.

"I never would've put us in this situation. This family is everything to me. It's all I fucking got. And if there was something that could risk all of us, I would've had no qualms about getting rid of it." He placed his hands on the desk and stared at me with his cold, dark eyes.

I knew he meant every word. Being the oldest, Cullen got the brunt of our father's abuse and aggression. Beatings, belittling, just an array of bullshit thrown his way. I knew Cullen had placed himself between us and our father, because he was protecting us. He'd shouldered a lot of shit, took the brunt of it to watch over us. And there was no doubt in my mind it had changed who he was.

No emotion, no fucks given. He did what he had to do and that was that. Even if that meant killing to protect us.

"Cullen, brother, I know your heart is in the right place, but I'm asking you to trust me and my judgment. I'm asking you, as my brother, to stand the fuck down." I didn't want to go toe-to-toe with him, but there was this marrow-deep need in me to protect Amelia.

Cullen didn't say anything. He just stood and shook his head slowly. "I hope she's fucking worth it, Dominik. Because if she rats us out or hurts any of us, I'll kill her whether you want her or not."

He left me standing there, letting his words play

through my head. I knew he meant every word he said. But in the back of my mind, I also knew that if this was what I wanted—with Amelia—I needed to make her irrevocably mine. I needed her to see she wasn't going anywhere.

Chapter Ten

Amelia

I didn't know what woke me, but I felt my eyes flutter open. I stared at the wall across from me for a suspended moment. Everything was quiet, still. Silent.

I don't know what had me sitting up and looking at the bedroom door, but as I did, the glow from the light filling the room in a soft hue, my heart started beating faster.

And then I heard him coming closer. Dom.

God, I feared him... but I was also excited he was close.

What was wrong with me?

And then the door opened. I don't know why a

surprised cry left me when I saw Dom standing there, the shadows covering the front half of him, his massive body impressive but also terrifying, because it told me exactly how much smaller I was than him. I moved back on the bed as if on instinct, as if my mind and body were at war with each other. I wanted to be closer to him… but I wanted to be farther away, because I knew how dangerous Dom really was.

He was dressed as if he were heading to bed or maybe sitting at the table getting wasted.

A pair of jeans that were unbuttoned at the waist, the denim loose and relaxed, faded and worn in. The white T-shirt he had on was a little on the wrinkled side, but it fit his massive body to perfection.

God, this man was intense in all the best ways.

He had a hand braced on the doorframe, his muscles so pronounced I actually felt a tingle move up my spine. I was aroused and he hadn't said anything, hadn't even moved.

I was off the bed, but at first I didn't know if I was going to retreat or move closer to him. I should have screamed, fought him off. He'd taken me.

No, he saved me. He saved me from his brother, who

would have put a bullet right in my head for just seeing his face.

I didn't have to be close to him to know he was drunk. I smelled it on him, saw the bottle of whiskey hanging from his grasp.

I wondered if I could get drunk just from the smell alone.

"I can't stop thinking of you," he said in a gravelly voice. It was deep and hoarse... masculine. It also sounded slightly slurred.

Hearing his words, his voice, made me even hotter, made me want to just give myself over right now.

What was wrong with me? Why did he have this effect on me? Why wasn't I fighting him tooth and nail to let me go?

Because you like this. You like the control, because your life so far has felt so out *of control.*

He didn't move, just stood there with his arm propped up on the doorframe, his bicep flexing. He was breathing hard and fast, as if he couldn't stop himself, couldn't control himself.

"What do you want?" I found myself whispering.

Did I really want to know though?

Dom stood there staring at me with half-lidded eyes, the desire on his face clear as day.

I felt it.

"What do I want?" he asked and took a step closer, coming into the room.

I didn't respond, didn't know how to. Because although he had said it like a question, the truth was I knew I already had the answer.

"You, Amelia. Isn't that clear?" He slowly closed the door, the light from the hallway extinguishing as he closed us in together.

My throat felt so tight. He was feet from me, blocking the exit, caging me in.

And I loved it. God help me, I wanted more.

I stared into his eyes, the whites bloodshot, glossy.

Was he high?

I smelled the alcohol on his breath and it turned me on more.

I was frozen in place, his words surrounding me, running through my head. He made everything else fade away, and it was like this drug, making me feel high, dizzy.

"I could have let you die back in that shop, could have let my brother snuff out your life."

"Then why didn't you?" I was poking a caged beast. I knew that, but I couldn't help myself.

He took another step forward... toward me.

"You. Because I wanted you." He took one more step closer, and I moved one back. I kept going until the wall stopped me from retreating, from running away. "And you want me."

I shook my head, but we both knew I was lying. I did want him. "I don't want you." Those words were whispered from me, a verbal admission that I was full of shit.

"Now you're gonna be a liar, Amelia?"

I didn't respond. I didn't know what to say to that. It was true. I was a liar in that moment.

He lifted a dark eyebrow and smirked, as if he found the whole thing funny. "Yeah, that's what I thought, baby."

The way he said that endearment had my heart dropping into my belly.

"I find it sexy as hell you got this twisted side to you, just like me."

"W-what do you mean?" God, why was my throat so dry?

He smirked again. "The fact that you're turned on right now, wet for a man who took you, who's keeping you prisoner in his home, because he wants you so fucking badly he doesn't care what laws he's breaking."

Dom took another step closer to me, then another and another until I smelled the masculine, spicy scent that surrounded him.

"You know what I want to do to you?"

I shook my head even though self-preservation said not to respond, not to fall prey to what this game was to him.

"I'll tell you, because I know you want to hear." He lowered his gaze to my mouth, and I forced myself not to lick my lips. "I want to fuck you until you can't walk straight." He lifted his eyes back to mine. "Not because that's all I want, but because it'll be me placing my claim on you. It'll be me making you mine, Amelia."

I placed my hands flat on the wall, the surface hard, the cold seeping into my body but doing nothing to chill the heat racing through me. The danger and violence that poured from Dom made me hotter, more excited.

I *was* wet, my nipples hard. This man could do whatever he wanted to me, and I wouldn't have a choice but to accept it all.

Liar. I'd accept it, because I wanted it. Bad.

Chapter Eleven

Amelia

God, my arousal rose like this ferocious, hungry animal. But at the same time, I was so turned on, so aroused that I felt crazed from it.

A part of me hated the fact that I was so turned on, but then again, I also didn't give a shit, because I'd never felt this way before. I'd never felt this kind of need. I'd never gone past kissing, never had anyone touch me... be with me.

I clenched my hands and shook my head, although I didn't know what I was trying to deny.

My need and desire for Dom? The fact that I was so wet my panties were soaked clean through?

And the sick truth was, the very thought of being kept here against my will made me even… hotter.

Dom was drunk and arrogant, thought he could have me simply because he deemed it so. Screw that. Fuck him.

Yes. Fuck him.

God, my thoughts were filthy.

"Just leave me alone," I whispered, but there was no heat or truth behind the words, no sincerity. I was so damn angry.

I craned my neck back so I could look into Dom's face. The masculinity that poured from him was so… potent.

He smirked and it made him even more attractive, if that was possible. I didn't know where he'd taken me, had only seen the inside of these four walls. It had been dark when we came here, and I'd been blindfolded when they pulled me out of the van. All I'd heard, seen, felt was the sound of my breathing, the race of the blood through my veins, and the beat of my pulse in my ears.

"It's amusing that you think you have any power in this situation, Amelia." He was staring at my mouth again. "But it turns me on even more than I find it funny."

We were closed in together, the smell of whatever dark and spicy cologne he wore, and the scent of the alcohol coming from him, filling the room and making me feel drunk.

"You're sick, keeping me here against my will. You're a bastard."

He smirked again and lifted his gaze to my eyes. "Against your will?" He lifted a dark brow. "Baby, you're not a prisoner. That door's been unlocked the whole time." He leaned in so close I couldn't think straight. All I wanted to do was close the distance between our mouths and kiss him.

But I wouldn't. I wanted him to close that gap, to take control like he had since the first moment I saw him in the jewelry store.

I opened my mouth, maybe to beg him to do just that or maybe to tell him to fuck off. But no words came out. I was frozen.

And then he was on me before I could even grasp what in the hell was going on. He used his upper body to push my back flush against the wall, a gasp leaving me, the air rushing out from my lungs.

"You want this. I want this. I'm done pretending I have any fucking self-control where you're concerned, Amelia." He had his hands on my waist, spun me around, and again, before I knew what was going on, he had me on the center of the bed.

"W-wait. What's going on? What are you doing?" I asked, even though I knew exactly what was happening.

Dom used his big body to press me against the mattress. My lips parted in shock… in lust when he wedged his hips between my thighs, the thick, very big and hard length of his erection rubbing against the most intimate, innocent part of me.

I was dizzy and lightheaded.

"If you honestly think I'm keeping you here against your will… you've gone off the deep end, baby girl." His voice was deep, low. "But then again, that would make you just as crazy as I am, and wouldn't that be a fucking match made in heaven."

"You don't know anything about me. You don't know what I want." I struggled to breathe, to speak. I was pretending like I wasn't affected, but it was all a damn lie.

He smirked, and it was darkly humorous. He didn't say anything in response, just pushed against me more until I felt his hardness. God, he was huge down there.

"Admit you're desperate for my cock. Admit it,

Amelia." He pressed his hips roughly against me, and an involuntary gasp left me.

"I'll never do that." Those words came out as a breath instead of a venomous retort.

He smirked. "I know I'm a motherfucker."

I let those words hang between us.

"But are you going to lie and say that tight little cunt of yours isn't wet for me, hungry for my dick?"

"You're insane. I won't ever admit that, tell you anything like that."

He leaned in close and I held my breath, waiting to see what he'd do in response to what I'd said.

But I wanted him to kiss me, wanted to feel his lips on mine, to just give in to Dom and let reality wash away.

Hadn't it already?

When our lips were only an inch apart, I turned my head, not wanting to give in to the twisted desires I felt for him. But the truth was I was so wet. God, I was soaked.

Dom gripped my chin and forced me to look at him again. "No, Amelia. You look me right in the eyes when we do this."

When we do this?

I felt his damn erection pressed against me. It was like a thick steel rod pressed right up against my pussy, as if trying to get inside me.

God… the thought of him inside me had my inner muscles clenching in need.

"Dammit, Amelia, baby." The way he groaned those words had my heart racing even harder. "I can feel how hot your pretty pussy is." He stared me right in the eyes. "If I placed my hand right on that bare cunt of yours, I bet you'd soak my hand, wouldn't you?"

"You're insane." Those words were low, hardly audible. But I knew he heard me, because he smirked.

He ground his erection into me, and I couldn't stop the gasp that left me.

Fuck him, and fuck the feelings I had for him.

His dick was pressed right up against my pussy, and even with layers of clothing separating us, I could feel how big it was.

What would he do if he knew I had never been with a man? Maybe he'd be disgusted, move away. Maybe he'd leave.

"I'm a virgin," I said quickly, the words spilling from me.

He pulled back and kept his focus on me. The expression on his face wasn't shocked, wasn't disgusted. He looked… pleased.

Chapter Twelve

Amelia

He stayed silent but had a look of pleasure, of satisfaction on his face.

Dom ground himself harder into me, rotating his hips so he bumped against the top of my mound, right on my clit.

"Music to my fucking ears, baby." He leaned in close again. "A virgin pussy. I'll be the one to pop that cherry, to claim it as mine."

A gasp of shock left me.

"I'll be the only one to ever know how hot and tight you are."

My traitorous body gave away my arousal, and I

wanted to scream, to push him away but bring him closer in the same breath.

I wish I was stronger than my emotions, but the truth was, I'd never felt this way. And I wanted more.

He pulled back and slowly let his gaze trail down to my chest. I had no doubt he could see how hard my nipples were. I felt like they'd tear through the material of my shirt.

"How long do you plan on keeping me here?" Those words spilled from me on a harsh whisper. I was breathing so damn hard. I hated I was betraying my strength with my arousal, my weakness.

The sight of his half-lidded gaze and the way his mouth was parted ever so slightly told me he was just as far gone as I was.

Then there was his rock-hard cock.

The gentle yet insistent thrusting of his hips between my legs, of his dick adding pressure right between her thighs, had me on the verge of getting off.

"However long I want, Amelia. I took you, because you're mine." He was still staring at my chest, his voice thick like he was drugged just from his arousal. He lifted his gaze back to my face. "Forever. I'll keep you forever, and you'll fucking love it."

I should have slapped him, pushed him off. His words were abrasive, so firm that it was hard not to believe him.

"No." I lied easily. Or at least I thought it was easy. That lone word was forced from me though.

"Go on. Keep fucking lying to me. It makes me want you even more."

"You can't keep me. This is illegal. You're breaking the law." I felt like an idiot for even saying those words. He didn't care about the law. He robbed Richard. He'd taken me.

"Baby, fuck the law. I do what I fucking want." His gaze was harsh and he leaned in closer, so close our noses almost touched. "And it's only illegal if I get caught."

A moment of silence passed between us, and then, shocking the hell out of me even more than he already had this entire time, he pressed his mouth on the side of my throat. I felt the scruff that covered his cheeks and jaw scratch at the sensitive skin of my throat, and a low moan left me. One of pleasure.

I felt my eyes close of their own accord. God, why did he have to affect me like this?

"Come on, Amelia," he said low, hauntingly demanding. "Ask me for it. Ask me for... me."

I shook my head but didn't know what I was saying no to. Him? My feelings? Trying to fight this?

He thrust against my pussy even more, running the tip of his tongue up and down the side of my throat. "I already told you that denying me only turns me on more." He had this wicked rhythm between my thighs now, the hard, massive length of his cock rubbing against my clit. I was going to come. I knew it. "Fucking ask me to take you."

Again, I shook my head. "No. Fuck you." Yeah, I actually said that, although I wasn't pushing him away.

"Look where your hands are, baby."

I had to force my eyes open, but when I did, I saw I was gripping his huge biceps, keeping him close.

"Look how wide your thighs are spread for me," he said as if pleased he could call me out.

And still he kept thrusting between my legs, our clothes stopping any penetration, any real, bare friction.

I was still staring at his biceps, where my hands were, where my nails were digging into him. He had tattoos covering one of his arms, his skin this golden color, his body so much bigger than mine.

"See how you're holding on to me?" he mumbled against my throat. "See how you're keeping me close?" He pulled back just enough that his mouth was by my ear now. "It's what I'm doing with you. It's why I took you." He was breathing so harshly. "I need you, and I can't fucking explain it. I don't understand why, but I won't give you back. I won't let you go, Amelia."

I turned my head so I was facing him. Our lips were so close I could have kissed him easily. Instead, I smiled slowly. "Fuck. You. Dom." It was the first time I'd said his name since he'd told me. It felt good to curse at him, to show him my strength.

Before I knew what was happening, he slammed his mouth on mine, pushing his tongue between the seam of my lips, invading, penetrating my mouth. I felt him shift atop me, his hand sliding between our bodies and stopping right at the waistband of my pants.

"Tell me to stop." It was a challenge. I knew it, heard it in his voice.

Somehow, I knew he'd stop if I told him to. But instead of saying that... I stayed silent.

He growled in pleasure right before he all but

ripped my pants down my legs. Dom was off me only long enough to take my shoes off and tear my pants completely off before tossing them aside. Then he was right back on me.

He pushed my thighs apart again, resting his big body against mine. He stayed fully clothed, and I didn't know why that aroused me even more. He had his mouth back on mine, fucking me there as he thrust his tongue in and out, claiming me.

And then he was reaching down and running his fingers along the edge of my panties, teasing and tormenting me in the same breath. Before I could contemplate what was going on, he slipped his fingers under the edge and touched my bare pussy.

He growled out again like some kind of feral animal. But then again, I guess he was. Feral. An animal.

"You're fucking soaked for me." He sounded so pleased with that fact. His denim-covered cock was pressed against my inner thigh. "You feel how hard you make me? Fuck, I've never been this hard before."

And when he started rubbing his fingers through my pussy, up and down my slit, this dark desire took hold. And I submitted, not fighting, not pretending I didn't want this.

"I bet you've lived a sheltered life, haven't you?" He all but groaned those words.

All I could do was shake my head.

A sheltered life was the last thing I'd had.

"Or maybe," he said and stared into my face again. "Maybe your life was just as fucked up as mine was."

And for the first time in my life... I felt like someone was looking at me who knew about me. Me.

And when he rubbed my clit, a gasp of pleasure left me, and all thought of the shitty life I'd had vanished.

"That's why I'm so drawn to you," he muttered and looked down at my lips. "One of the reasons anyway." He continued to touch me, torment me. "You and I are one and the same." I found myself actually lifting my hips, seeking his touch, that pleasure. "That's it. Keep silently begging for it." He hummed in approval. "If I keep touching this hot little pussy of yours, will you come for me, Amelia? Will you give me what I've been dreaming of since I first saw you?"

I opened my mouth, maybe to say no or to tell him I would be his, but no words came out. Instead, I mewled like a greedy bitch.

My orgasm was right there at the surface, threatening to break free. His focus was on me the entire time, his eyes locked on mine, the controlled expression on his face so damn attractive. Surrendering to him seemed so right, like it was exactly what I should do.

"Just give in to me, baby," he said gruffly.

And it was as if his words had everything else fading away.

"Give me what I want. Come for me." He touched my slit with more intention, rubbed me harder. He ground his cock against my inner thigh in time with those touches until I felt my orgasm start to build.

Closing my eyes again, I curled my nails into his hard, warm flesh, knowing it probably hurt him but not caring.

"That's it," he whispered and never stopped rubbing me. His alcohol-laced breath slid along my lips and I inhaled, wanting to take that intoxication into my body… wanting to take *him* into my body. He applied just a little bit of pressure, and I felt tendrils of an orgasm rising violently to the surface.

Oh my God. Was I really going to get off for him? Was I really going to come for the man who kidnapped me?

"You going to come for me?" He phrased it like a question, but I could hear the approval, the fact that he already knew the answer, in his voice.

I didn't answer, didn't give him the satisfaction of a response.

Survival kicked in and I pushed at his arms, but it was weak, futile, because the truth was, I didn't want to push him away. I wanted to bring him closer.

Dom was so strong, so powerful that I just went with it, not because he forced me, but because I desperately wanted this.

I needed this to go on, this pleasure, this detachment from reality.

God, I was going to come so hard.

"That's it, Amelia. Just give me what I want." He ground against me over and over again, and my eyes nearly rolled back in my head. "Just surrender and give yourself what you want."

And then, as if his words were a soothing balm, that little push I needed, everything faded away as I felt my orgasm finally peak. Closing my eyes again, I curled my nails into his hard, warm flesh and let the world vanish.

"This is crazy," I whispered, not realizing I said the words out loud.

Dom kept rubbing my clit, prolonging my pleasure, drawing it out as if he couldn't help himself, as if he knew exactly what I wanted and desperately desired.

God, I never wanted this to end.

As Dom kept thrusting his cock against my inner thigh, the hardness of it so big and impressive, so intimidating, all I could do was let the world fade away and enjoy this. I couldn't suck air into my lungs, couldn't let my sanity fade away.

I heard him groan, knew he felt the same intense desire as I did.

Dom picked up his pace, rocking his hips back and forth against me, his hand still between my thighs as he stared right in my eyes.

"Yes," I said out loud and felt my face heat in embarrassment.

I felt another tremor of ecstasy move through me, and then I was gasping for air, grinding my pussy against his fingers.

He pulled his hand from between my legs and held up his fingers, the glossiness that covered them making me feel uneasy, because I knew they were that wet because of how aroused I was. "You see how worked up you are for me?" He brought the digits to his mouth but didn't slip them inside just yet. "I bet you taste fucking incredible, don't you, baby?"

I couldn't answer. What was I supposed to say to that? What could I say?

He didn't need a response from me, not when he sucked his fingers into his mouth and cleaned them, taking my essence into his body.

The sight had a wave of pleasure coursing through me.

"God. Fuck yes." Dom said those words on a harsh whisper, closing his eyes for a second to savor my flavor on his tongue. "*Fuck.*" He moved away from me, as if tearing his body from mine, as if I burned him.

I couldn't move, didn't want to. He stood, had his back to me for a second, and then ran his hand over his hair, his muscles flexing and bunching from the act.

There was no denying the atmosphere changed, the room becoming cold, the air seeming thicker. He glanced at me, and I lowered my gaze to his crotch, saw how hard he still was, felt my eyes widen as I saw a wet spot starting to form on the denim from the obvious pre-cum seeping through the material.

His expression was hard, his body stiff. He

looked angry, or maybe he was conflicted. I knew I was the latter for sure.

Without saying anything to me, he reached out, grabbed the door handle, and left, closing the door behind him and leaving me feeling like an emptiness now consumed me.

I knew what I'd just done, what I'd let Dom do to me, would forever change everything.

I didn't know if that scared me… or if I was looking forward to more.

Chapter Thirteen

Amelia

I slowly opened my eyes, drowsiness trying to claim me again. I rolled over, knowing I was still alone, feeling the lack of Dom's presence in the room.

It felt devoid.

I felt devoid.

I stared at the bedroom door, the same one Dom had exited, the one that closed me in after he made me come several times. My body was pleasantly sore despite the fact that we hadn't actually had sex.

The remembrance of him grinding against me, of his mouth on mine, the scruff on his cheeks abrading the sensitive skin at my throat, had arousal moving through me once more. My nipples hardened and a shiver worked its way up my spine.

I realized I was under the covers, my body bare of any clothing except for my bra, the sweat already having dried on me. I didn't remember getting under the covers. Had he come back?

In the flurry of activity with Dom, my clothes had been discarded, while he had stayed fully dressed. I found that arousing as hell, far more exciting than if he'd gotten undressed himself, just as stark naked as I had been.

I grabbed the sheet and held it up to my chest as I slowly sat up, the scent of him all around me— on my skin, in my hair, on the very sheets that surrounded me. It was then I noticed a stack of clothes at the edge of the bed. A pair of sweats and a shirt. His.

He had come back in here after I'd fallen asleep.

I looked at that bedroom door again and swallowed roughly, glancing at my pile of clothes on the floor, knowing it was smart if I would've just put those on, but instead I reached for his garments.

I slipped his shirt on, the material so big on me, my body tiny compared to it. And then I put on the sweats, pulled the drawstring as far as it would go, and tied it in a knot. But it was still too big, and so I rolled the waistband down, keeping the material in place as much as I could.

I glanced down at myself, my body swimming in the fabric. I felt very intimate at this moment, very close with Dom even though I was alone. I knew nothing about him, not anything that wasn't on the surface, easily seen, readily visible. I had no idea how old he was, what his last name was. I didn't know what his mother and father were like, if he'd had a happy childhood or one like mine.

Hell, I didn't even know where he lived. I didn't know where I was. Yet here I was, wearing his clothing, and the memory of his body on top of mine as he worked himself on me until I orgasmed for him playing through my mind.

He made me come more than once, and that played on repeat in my head, like a broken record that I didn't want to correct.

I gathered the front of his shirt and brought it up to my nose, inhaling deeply. There was a spicy, almost evergreen aroma to the material. Wild. Feral.

I looked at the bedroom door again, knowing what I had to do, what I should do. And I found myself walking toward it, opening it, staring out into a living room and a kitchen. We were in the basement, if descending stairs when I first got here was anything to go by.

The living room was fully finished, an apartment all on its own. I was frozen in place, afraid he'd catch me, that something bad would happen. But I didn't feel fear. I was curious.

I stepped farther into the living room. To my left was a leather couch directly in front of the flat screen TV that was mounted to the wall. To my right was a computer desk, the laptop on it closed. My heart was thundering as I walked over to it and opened it, not knowing what I was going to do, if I was going to try to contact somebody for help, or to see if Richard was okay, or if there was any news about the robbery. But it was password-protected, and the time I would've spent trying to figure out how to get on it—which I probably wouldn't have been able to do anyway—wasn't something I was going to mess with.

I closed the laptop and looked around for a phone, although the truth was, who would I have called? Richard? The police? The very thought of turning Dom in twisted my stomach, had confusion racing through me. What in the hell was wrong with me?

But there was no phone. No cell, not a landline. Nothing.

I walked over to the kitchen, looking at a standard-sized fridge, opening it up. Beer, some condiment bottles, a pizza box.

Vassillia Pizzeria.

I had never heard of that company, so I clearly wasn't still in town.

I closed the fridge and looked around. White marble counters were a contrast to the black cupboards. Everything was sleek and very minimalistic. I noticed there were no pictures, nothing hanging on the walls, no decorations of any sort. It was like an empty slate, a blank pallet.

Then again, Dom didn't seem like the type of guy who lavished himself in materialistic things.

And then I saw the door, the one I presumed led upstairs. My heart was racing as I walked to it, gripped the handle and turned it, pulling the door open. There was a small tile foyer right before the stairs, and as I stood there, staring up the length of them, seeing the door that would lead to an escape, I actually found myself taking a step back.

I reached out and grabbed the banister of the stairs, taking that first step almost hesitantly, tentatively. "What in the fuck is wrong with me?" I whispered those words to myself as I started to ascend, each step taking me closer and closer to freedom. Although I didn't really know if that was actually the case. For all I knew, there was a guard standing right on the other side of that door with a gun, just waiting for me to open it so he could put a bullet between my eyes.

The image of the one named Cullen flashed through my mind, and I felt a chill race over me. He was frightening and calm, collected and dangerous. I could tell he had no issues about killing. And his eyes... his eyes were dead, no emotion coming from them.

I found myself taking steps backward, turning and going right back to the only place I'd felt safe since I'd been here. And for the hundredth time since I'd been brought here, I thought how crazy I was. Maybe I was weak, conditioned from childhood that there was no hope, no clawing my way out from under the shit that my life was buried in.

Maybe I was just so used to being fucked over that this was normal, that any ounce of comfort and attention I got was something to be celebrated, latched on to. But as soon as those thoughts slammed into my mind, I immediately pushed them away. They felt foreign and wrong, because what I felt for Dom—the strange and exciting, exhilarating, and almost frightening emotions I had for him —wasn't something I'd ever felt in my life.

It wasn't something I'd ever thought I would feel. Although it wasn't love, wasn't just lust either, it was this connection I felt when I looked at him, when he touched me and spoke to me. It was as if he knew me, as if his soul knew what it was like to live my life, to be in my situation.

It was as if we were the same person.

Instead of doing what I should have done, what was the smart thing, I went back to his bedroom, shut the door, and walked over to the bed. I kept my back to the door, thinking, not sure what was wrong with me, but knowing what I was doing was the right thing to do, no matter what the "realistic" thing was, no matter what anyone thought.

Or maybe there wasn't anything wrong with me at all. Maybe everything was right.

Chapter Fourteen

Cullen

She was a piece of ass. That's all it was. This golden pussy my brother couldn't help keeping for himself. I understood the possessiveness that came from Dom. Hell, we'd all felt it at one time or another during our fucked-up lives. When you didn't have shit growing up, you tended to get territorial real easy.

But Dom was blinded by his need for her, his arousal. He didn't understand she was a liability, a risk to all of us. She'd seen our faces, and the fact was she could ID us to the cops. Hell, she worked at the fucking jewelry store we just robbed. I didn't know what it was about her that drew him so irrevocably to her, but that line needed to be broken, that tether severed.

And I was going to be the one to cut it.

I should have left the house as soon as we talked about the job and payout. I should have pulled myself away from the dark temptation to finish her off and "save" my brother. Instead, I'd stayed. And that had been a mistake.

I heard Dom head out to the garage to work out and could practically smell the desire that came from him. I didn't know if he'd fucked her yet, but if he had, it would make things even more complicated. A Preacher boy claimed hard—that was for damn sure.

Although none of us had ever claimed a woman, whatever we set our mind to we did it with everything in us. It's why we were the way we were, why we were so good at our job. It was why being professional fucking thieves came so natural to us.

When we were focused, that was it… all bets were off, nothing could deter us. And that's what Dom's issue was now.

I'd handle it, and after it was all said and done, he'd see it was better this way, that I'd done him and all of us a favor.

I headed down to the basement, and when I

reached the landing, I cocked my head to the left and looked at Dom's closed bedroom door. He didn't even fucking lock anything, not the door that led upstairs, and I knew for a fucking fact that the bedroom door was currently unlocked.

And although she wouldn't have been able to escape, not while I was here, this lack of concern he had regarding her pissed me off. He was too lenient with her, trusted her, because he wanted between her legs.

I walked toward the door and stopped in front of it, listening. It was silent, and I imagined her sleeping, curled up in the center of his bed, unaware of the monster who stood just feet from her, only a slab of wood protecting her from me.

I reached out and grabbed the handle, turning it and then pushing the door open. I saw her sitting on the edge of the bed, her back to me, her head slightly downcast. Because of the angle, I couldn't see exactly what she was doing, but I assumed she was looking at her hands, thinking about her situation, worrying.

She was probably terrified, as she should be.

I took a step into the room and I saw her back straighten, her head lifting slightly, but still she didn't turn around and face me.

"I wondered when you'd come back," she said softly, no fear in her voice.

Did she know it was me standing right behind her, a loaded gun in my hand, intending to kill her?

I didn't say anything, and she didn't turn around.

"I've been thinking about what we did, how I feel." I heard a tremor of desire in her voice for my brother. She inhaled and then exhaled slowly. "This is crazy, Dom. I'm insane for how I feel for you." That last part was whispered, but I heard it all the same.

I didn't say anything, didn't feel anything but my one goal, my one task. And that was to finish this so she didn't ruin our lives.

I didn't care how my brother felt for her. I didn't give a fuck what she thought she felt for Dom. This family was everything to me, and she wasn't a part of that. She wasn't a part of the plan.

"But what I know for sure, even through all of this, how ludicrous all of this is, Dom…" She paused, maybe thinking about what to say next, maybe regretting all of this. "What I know is that the very thought of leaving, of not being with you, makes me feel… unfulfilled. It scares me."

I could hear the passion and sincerity in her

voice, the genuine emotion she felt. I never understood those who let their raw emotions control
them. Love was nothing more than a chemical reaction. It was fleeting, extinguishable. It was easy
enough to turn off and on.

"And I don't know what all this means, Dom. I
don't. I'm stupid for feeling anything more than
hatred and fear for you. But the way you touch me,
the things you said to me—whispered—makes me
feel like this isn't the worst thing I'll ever do in my
life." She inhaled sharply. "It makes me feel like this
is exactly where I'm supposed to be."

She turned around then, a small, almost hopeful
smile on her face as if a weight had been lifted off
of her for saying the words. But when she came
face-to-face with me, her smile faltered and her eyes
widened.

Fear.

Realization that this was over for her.

She was afraid, and that immediately took root,
covering her expression, changing the air around us.
It grew frigid, cold.

I said nothing as I stared at her, watched how
her body instantly reacted, how her flight-or-fight
instinct rose up. She lowered her gaze and looked at

my hand, the one that held the gun, the weapon that would end her life.

"Wait. Wait, please." She stammered the words out, stumbled over them. She backed away from me, but the wall stopped her retreat. I stepped inside, went closer to her, my cock rock-hard. Then again, it didn't take much effort to do that.

She was searching the room for a way out, but the only escape was the door behind me. She'd have to get through me to get there, and that wasn't going to happen. She was small, tiny really. I could see the appeal she had for Dom, the fact that she was so feminine, the dark-red hair, the big green eyes. She had a petite frame, but I could see her womanly curves.

Yeah, I could see the attraction, but fucking a woman, getting your dick wet, was a hell of a lot different than keeping her as some kind of treasure.

I was right in front of her now, staring down at her, seeing her big eyes staring up at me with fear and the realization that this was it. But as I looked into her eyes, I felt something shift in me. I thought about what she said, how she said it. I thought about what she must feel for Dom, that she sounded like it was so... true.

"You think you have feelings for my brother?" I tipped my head slightly to the side, examining her. Although she didn't cry, I knew she was on the verge. But she was strong, and I had to give her credit for that.

She was strong. But she wasn't stronger than me.

She didn't answer right away, but I saw the way her throat worked as she swallowed, could see in her expression she was thinking about my question.

"I-I don't know." I liked her honesty. "But I know what I feel for him seems... right." The last part was said almost too softly for me to hear.

She ran her hands up and down her thighs, and it was the first time I realized she was wearing Dom's clothes, a pair of oversized sweats and a white T-shirt, both far too big for her. She was swimming in the material.

"You think I'll tell, turn you in." She shook her head. "I won't."

"You might," I said evenly, calmly.

She shook her head again, the determination on her face more evident now. "I won't." The way she whispered that had a lot of strength behind it.

For the first time since this all started, since I

knew what I had to do where she was concerned, I actually found myself questioning whether this was really the best option. Who was I to stand in the way of one of my brothers getting what they wanted? We'd had nothing growing up, nothing given to us but beatings and lessons on how to steal and survive.

But one of my brothers actually happy, getting something they really wanted? Well fuck, that almost made my cold, dead heart warm.

I leaned in close and stared into her big green eyes. "You know it would be so easy for me to find you if you ran." I let that really sink in. "It would be so damn easy to know what rock you crawled under to get away from me if you tried to turn us in." She didn't move, didn't even breathe. "It would be too fucking easy to sneak into your bedroom at night and wrap my hand around your pretty little throat and squeeze the life from you." Despite the fact that I knew she was terrified, she stayed still and calm, didn't outwardly show her fear.

I had to give her credit.

"I won't tell anyone about you or this, because… because of how I feel for Dom."

I lifted a brow at that.

But before I could say anything, before I could lift the gun I held and point it right between her eyes—if I would have done that in the end anyway —I heard someone racing down the stairs.

Not just anyone... but Dom.

Chapter Fifteen

Dom

I 'd known something was wrong when I'd seen the basement door open, and then I felt the coldness fill the air.

Cullen.

I knew he wouldn't have let this be. It wasn't who he was, wasn't his nature.

And when I'd rushed to my room, expecting the worst, ready to go toe-to-toe with my brother for taking away from me the only good thing to ever come into my life, my heart had jumped to my throat.

Everything in me stilled when I saw Amelia

pressed against the wall, her eyes wide as she stared at Cullen.

My brother was only a few feet away from her, and although I couldn't see his expression, I saw the way his head was cocked. He was examining her, his thought process obvious as he no doubt considered what to do next.

And when I saw the gun in his hand, time stood still. I couldn't react quick enough.

And then he slowly turned his head in my direction, a slow smile spreading across his face as if he knew what I was thinking, as if he had no fucking issues with being caught with my woman, a gun in his hand, the air cold and menacing around him.

I didn't think. I just reacted.

I was on him the next second, ripping him away from Amelia, slamming his body against the opposite wall. I heard her gasp, but I had to focus on Cullen, on stopping this. After that was done, I'd go to her, comfort her, make sure Cullen hadn't touched a hair on her head.

Cullen was a big fucker, tall and muscular... the biggest out of the four of us. The sound of his body hitting the wall seemed to fill the entire room. And still, the asshole grinned.

I felt my anger arise, my rage growing because

he'd been here, the threat of what he was going to do a reality.

"I warned you," I growled harshly, my voice nothing more than a serrated tone from me. "I fucking warned you, Cullen. I told you to stay away from her. She's mine." I charged forward, slamming my fist into his jaw, his head cracking to the side from the impact.

He didn't fight me back, although I knew if he did this would've been one bloody fucking match. Instead, he stood there, his dark eyes hard, his gaze intent.

"We don't fucking kill people, Cullen." I said those words again, repeating them like when I'd spit them out in the garage just the night before. "We don't fucking go after a brother's female." I stared at him right in the eyes, my emotions turbulent in that moment. I was letting him know with my body language and with my words, expression, and actions that she was mine.

She was my woman.

"I told you to stay away." My voice was pained as I stared at my big brother. "Why couldn't you just leave it be? Why couldn't you trust me to make the right call?" I shook my head, my forearm still at his throat. "I told you not to touch her or there would be repercussions." I curled my other hand into a fist, and before I knew it was happening, I slammed my knuckles into his temple.

And still, he didn't fight back.

He grunted in pain, his body shifting across the wall from the impact. I split his cheek, the gash running across his cheekbone, a trail of blood sliding down. My knuckles throbbed, bled. They'd be bruised and swollen in the morning. But it wouldn't matter. This was going to be painful for both of us in more ways than one.

"I'm protecting you, all of us," he finally said.

"You couldn't stay away, could you?" I phrased it like a question, although I didn't expect an answer. I didn't want one from him. "You couldn't give me this, huh? Couldn't let things be."

Cullen looked at me again, and I saw that coldness directed right at me. He snarled and spit out a mouthful of blood and saliva. "We don't fucking fall for a female on the job. We're professional fucking thieves, Dom. We don't kidnap women and keep them as damn pets."

She wasn't a pet. She was mine.

But I didn't say that, not again. I couldn't say anything in response, because Cullen was right to an extent. But when I'd seen Amelia, something in me had snapped. All I'd felt was possessiveness, this territorial need to make her mine. It was insane, fucking ludicrous. But damn, it felt real, and so all I'd done was react.

"This is it, Cullen. This is the only chance I'm giving you, your last saving grace. You're my brother, which is the only reason I'm not fucking killing you right now. But brother or not, Amelia is mine. If you touch her again, I will walk away. From you. From the family. From everything."

I saw a flash of something filter across Cullen's face, but it was gone before I could really gauge what it meant.

Regret?

Surprise?

Disappointment?

I'd never know, because Cullen was a fortress when it came to what he felt and thought.

The fact that I had to tell Cullen this was painful. It took a little piece of me, stole a part of my life. He was my big brother, had always had my back. And walking away from him, away from everything, scared the hell out of me. It was foreign, like someone was reaching in and taking a piece of my identity. But this was my life, what I wanted. Amelia was mine, and if Cullen couldn't see that, couldn't respect it, then there was no place for me here.

There was no doubt in my mind that this would be the right choice, that it was exactly what I was supposed to do, what I'd always been meant to do.

I looked over my shoulder and saw she stood still by the wall, her arms wrapped around her waist, her eyes wide. She looked frightened, but she also had strength within her, this part of her that drew me to her like a moth to a flame. She was fiery, had a spark of life in her. And the light that came from her illuminated the darkness within me. I knew she had been put into my life for a reason, that it was fate, destiny, whatever the fuck you wanted to call it.

Our paths crossing was no mistake.

I looked back at Cullen, waiting for his answer. He showed no emotion, but I was used to that. We all were. He would've been classified as a sociopath, I was sure. But whether he was or wasn't, I didn't care. He was my brother, family, blood. And the only reason I hadn't put a bullet between his eyes for going against what I said and threatening Amelia was because we were family.

I took a step back and waited, the rage still

burning through my veins. Cullen moved away from the wall and glanced over at Amelia.

"No." That word came out of me harshly. "You don't fucking look at her. You look at me, Cullen." I said that last part sternly, making it known where I was in the situation.

Cullen slowly looked back at me, this smirk coming out once more. "You're about to risk everything for a woman? You want to put our lives in jeopardy, all because you have this obsession, this fixation with some pussy?"

I took a step forward, about to slam my fist into his face for talking about Amelia like that, but then I stopped myself and looked back at Amelia.

She still had wide eyes as she shook her head, as if knowing fighting with Cullen wouldn't solve anything. It would make it worse.

I turned back and looked at my brother. Still, he said nothing. Still, he looked stone-cold, like the killer he was.

And then I saw something change in him, his expression shifting, his look hardening impossibly more.

"You want to fucking risk everything for some piece of ass, then have at it, brother." Cullen stepped closer to me, and I felt a shot of cold air come from him. "But when shit hits the fan and I have to be the one to handle things, again, don't come at me." He stared me in the eyes, cold and hard, unforgiving. "Because I'll do whatever it takes to make sure we aren't fucked over." Cullen looked at Amelia for a second before snapping his attention back to me. "And you know I will. You know I won't have any issues taking out the problem, Dominik."

With that, he turned and left, leaving Amelia and me alone, the air so damn thick because of Cullen, but becoming more manageable, breathable now that he was gone. I turned and faced Amelia, seeing her still pressed to the wall, hating that she was in this situation, was feeling this way because of me.

This was my fault.

"Amelia."

She didn't move, didn't speak as I stepped closer. I wanted to hold her, to touch her, to make sure she was okay after all this.

"I'm sorry," I whispered gruffly, my throat dry, my body feeling so damn tight I might snap. Amelia pushed away from the wall and stepped closer to me. We stared at each other for long seconds, and before I knew what I was doing, I had her in my arms, her body pressed to mine. I had one hand wrapped around her nape, tilted her head back an inch, and all I wanted to do was stake my claim, mark her, let her know I'd do anything for her.

I stroked my tongue along the seam of her lips, urging her to open, fucking hoping like hell she'd give in to me fully, let me touch her, feel her, thrust deep inside her. And then she opened for me, a little gasp leaving her. I swallowed it, took it into myself, loving the way she pressed her body to mine, her breasts thrust against my chest.

"That's it," I groaned and kissed her harder, moving my tongue in and out of her mouth like I wanted to do with my cock between her thighs. "You taste so fucking good," I groaned again and walked her backward until the wall stopped our movements. I slid my hands down her arms and curled my fingers against hers then dragged them up, rubbing them along the wall and keeping them in place above her head. I wrapped one hand around both of her wrists, her body spreading for me like an offering. I stepped back and looked down at her. "God, you're fucking gorgeous."

Moving a lock of her hair over her shoulder, I saw her body tense a second before her cheeks became pink. She blushed for me, and it was the prettiest fucking thing. When she looked up at me, her eyes were wide with arousal and… surprise.

"I'd never let anything or anyone hurt you," I whispered and looked at her lips.

"You don't know me," she whispered back.

I lifted my gaze and stared into her eyes. "But I do, Amelia. I know you like I know myself." We looked at each other, and I felt the air in the room become hotter, felt my cock throb behind my jeans. I wanted to just say fuck it all and kiss her again until she was breathless.

"God. I can't breathe."

Yeah, neither could I.

I felt a chill race up my spine, felt my balls draw up tight as I heard her inhale sharply as I saw the way her pupils dilated, her mouth part. Her lips were red and glossy from my kiss.

Something snapped inside me. I wrapped one of my hands around her waist, pulled her right up against my body once more, and curled the fingers of my other hand around the nape of her neck. For long seconds, I just held her, loving the way she molded against me.

"I want you," I said. "And I want you to want me with the same intensity, Amelia. I need that." I held my breath as I waited for her response, as I thought about what she'd say, what she might not say.

She could deny me, say no, that she didn't want me, but the truth was I wouldn't stop until she was mine. She could run. She could hide. But I'd always find her.

And when she licked her lips and nodded, I felt my smile of satisfaction grow.

Nothing else mattered but being with Amelia in every way.

Chapter Sixteen

Amelia

Dom had my back pressed to the wall once again, and I sucked in a deep breath, the air cold in my lungs. I didn't try to push him away. I wanted this like I wanted to take another breath.

Was it wrong that I was aroused right now, wet for Dom, ready to take him into my body? Ready to have him claim my virginity? Was it wrong to want a man who had kidnapped me, who had a brother who wanted me dead?

Or maybe this is right where I am supposed to be.

"I want you, this, Dom."

Dominik made this deep sound in the back of

his throat, his focus going down to my chest. I felt my nipples harden, felt how sensitive my breasts were because of how much desire I felt. My emotions were running high right now, and I looked down as well, saw in embarrassment that yes, my nipples stabbed through the white T-shirt.

My body was showing him exactly what it wanted… who I wanted.

And that was Dom. Now.

He smoothed his hand down my inner arm and stopped at my wrists, placing his fingers right over my pulse point. Could he feel how fast it was beating for him? 'Cause it felt like a fucking derailed train inside me.

He applied a little pressure, and his touch was intimate, electrifying.

"Amelia, once I start this, there's no going back." He stared right in my eyes. "But honestly, there was no going back once I saw you in that jewelry store." He looked at my mouth. "You'll be mine in all ways."

I became lightheaded.

Every erogenous zone in my body tingled at the way he looked at me, at what he said. My pussy became wetter with each passing moment.

He placed his hands by my head and leaned in

again, this deep, low sound leaving him. His nostrils flared, and he looked down at my breasts once more. It was like he was touching me with his sight alone.

Touch me. Kiss me. Be with me.

I felt drunk, intoxicated from my need. I knew I didn't want this to stop. Never. His gaze was penetrating, like he reached out and stroked my skin, touched every part of me. I started to tremble from my emotions, from the excitement and anticipation moving through my veins. This little voice inside my head told me I should feel sick, wrong, because I wanted this with a man like Dominik.

"Get undressed for me, Amelia. Show me all of you again."

I didn't even hesitate as I did exactly what he wanted.

And when I was naked, bared for him, I watched as he looked his fill of me.

"So fucking gorgeous." His voice dropped an octave, and a chill raced up my spine.

I knew what I was doing would forever change me, but what I didn't know was if it would ruin me or change me for the better.

He took a step back and ran a hand over his mouth as he looked at my body, his gaze moving up and down, his eyes now trained on my pussy. He slid his gaze up to my chest, and I swore I knew his mouth watered.

"Look at those perfect tits."

I started to sweat, beads forming on my entire body, between my breasts, down the length of my spine. And I was wet, my pussy so soaked for him that when he did slide into me, the motion would be fluid, easy. Perfect.

"I want you," he finally said, and I swallowed. His voice was a husky growl, one that sounded more animal than man. "You want me?"

I nodded, not trusting myself to speak.

He reached down and lewdly gripped himself through his jeans. "You see how hard I am for you, how much I want you?"

The fact that I felt so alive with Dom scared the hell out of me. Wanting him terrified me. But it was my desire for him that controlled everything right now.

And it was that uncertainty, that fear, that excited me the most.

He took a step toward me until he was only a few inches away from me. Dom reached out and cupped my chin with his forefinger and thumb. For long seconds, he didn't say anything, didn't move, didn't even breathe. He just gently held my chin and stared at my lips. The air around us was hot, charged with lust.

"You're trembling, baby," he whispered.

Yeah, I was.

"Are you afraid of me?"

I shook my head right away. "No."

"Then why are you shaking?"

"Because of how much I want you."

He hummed low and leaned in so his lips were close to mine. "That's what I like to fucking hear, but admit it, baby. Admit you're kind of afraid of how this is all going."

I was silent for long seconds. I wouldn't lie to him. I'd always tell him the truth, even if that truth could fuck everything up.

He slid his free hand along my side, over my outer thigh, and around to cup my ass. My pussy tingled, and my clit throbbing in time with my pulse. He'd barely touched me and I felt like I was on the verge of coming.

"Do you like this?" He gave my ass a squeeze and moved his other hand, the one that had been holding my chin, down my chest to cup one of my breasts. "You like what I'm doing to you? Touching you?"

"God. Yes." Shit, I sounded like I was begging.

He ran his fingers over my areola, along my hard little nipple. He never once looked away from me as he cupped my breasts, tweaked the tip until I curled my toes. He made this deep, gruff sound in the back of his throat.

"Say my name when you say you want this."

Another gasp of pleasure left me.

"I want you, Dom." I closed my eyes and breathed through the sensations.

"Damn, baby. Hearing you say that could make me come right now."

And then Dom had me in his arms, both of his hands cupping my ass. He turned and strode toward the bed. I knew that without even seeing, knew that from the focused intent on his face, in the way he touched me.

I was on the mattress as the world spun, and I felt flushed with need. The sheets were cold against my overheated flesh, and I reached out and gripped them, curling my hands into the soft material.

And then I watched as he got undressed, as he looked at me the entire time. I felt like prey to a very dangerous predator. I was primed for him, so ready for his big cock.

Once he was naked, I lowered my gaze to his

crotch. My pussy clenched with the need to be filled by him, to see how much pain and pleasure there would be trying to fit all of that into my body.

"Spread your fucking legs for me. Let me see how wet your cunt is."

I didn't even think of disobeying. I braced her feet flat on the bed, spread wide until my pussy lips parted for him, and held my breath as I waited for him to respond, to react.

He didn't speak, just kept his focus on my pussy and stepped closer until he was at the edge of the bed. For a second, he was frozen in place, but then he reached out and smoothed his fingers through my slit. I cried out in pleasure.

Dom slid his fingers to my clit and added pressure. I arched my back, needing more.

He moved even closer until he was on the bed now, leaning over me, above me. His body was so muscular that he blocked out everything behind him. And then he was lowering himself between my legs, his mouth… God, his mouth was so close to my pussy that his warm breath had my inner muscles clenching.

"You ever have anyone taste this sweet little pussy?"

I closed my eyes and shook my head. "No. Never."

"Good."

A shiver worked through me. I made a soft sound in the back of my throat, not caring that the noise had left me, that I sounded desperate. His mouth was right over my pussy, but he didn't lick me, didn't move his tongue along that sensitive part, even though I ached for him to do just that. Instead, he moved his body up mine until his mouth was right over my nipple. I arched my back, trying to thrust my chest against his mouth. Dom groaned and ran his tongue over the hard tip.

"Amelia."

The way he said my name was so arousing, like he couldn't survive without me.

"You see how you are for me? So fucking primed and ready to take my big cock in your tight little pussy?"

All I could do was nod.

Over and over, he moved his tongue along the peak of my nipple, sucking on the flesh, tugging at it with his teeth, bringing me close to orgasm from that act alone. He sucked on my nipple harder, and I couldn't help but bite my lip in response. I was going to climax from the act alone, from having him so close, from having him touch me and want me so furiously.

And I had no intentions of stopping it from happening. He sucked harder and faster, groaned against the flesh until vibrations went right to my clit.

"Dominik."

"Say my fucking name again, Amelia. Say it like you're dying for me."

I gasped. "Dom. God. Dom, more. I need more."

He groaned and smoothed his fingers between my pussy folds. I felt my back bow in response, my flesh pressing against his mouth even more.

More. I needed so much more.

Chapter Seventeen

Amelia

He was a dirty talker, and I hadn't known how much I wanted that, needed that until I heard him saying those things.

He slipped his fingers against my folds. "Fuck, you're so fucking soaked, baby." He settled his lips at the crook of my neck, gently pulling at her flesh with his teeth. He had his hand between my legs still, lazily stroking my pussy, rubbing his fingers against my clit.

"I want more," I said with desperation in my voice.

A low, needy groan left him, and he added more pressure to my clit.

"Yes," I cried out when he rubbed the little bud harder, moving his finger around it faster, using my lubrication in his motions.

"You want to come?" When I nodded, he added, "Touch me."

I obeyed instantly and placed my hands on his wide, strong shoulders, wanting him closer, needing him closer.

He didn't stop rubbing his fingers against my clit, tormenting me over and over, giving me pleasure mixed with pain.

"I want to take my time, but I also need to fuck you." He bit at my throat, the pain slight, the pleasure monumental. I was beginning to realize how controlled Dom was, how demanding in getting what he wanted.

I ached for more, was desperate for it to last forever. There was no doubt I felt exposed, every part of me tender and sensitive.

"More," I actually found myself saying before I could stop myself.

He used his body to press closer against me, making me sink more into the mattress. His face was so close to mine once again. I wanted to breathe the same air, be one with each other.

"The fact that I'm the one making you feel this

good, that I'll be the one popping that cherry and forever claiming it, has me so damn territorial over you, Amelia." He ground his erection into my belly, over and over again. "You feel how hard you make me?"

"God, yes." Dom's cock was hot and huge. I was actually a little timid to have him pushing that monster into me. But I also anticipated it.

He moved back a few inches and slid his hands down my thighs, over my knees, and curled his fingers around my calves. I looked down at the third fucking arm he was sporting. God. Massive.

He was so big… everywhere. And I felt so small compared to him.

God, I couldn't think straight, couldn't even breathe because of all the pleasure, all the sensations moving through me.

I'd been taken by this man, but all I wanted to do was give myself over to him irrevocably. The truth was, being with Dominik was exciting, maybe even a little bit dangerous. No, not a little bit. A lot. He was dangerous, a criminal. But that turned me on even more.

For the first time in my life, I wasn't going to worry about anything else but being with Dominik and feeling the intense pleasure he gave me.

"God, you giving into me is so fucking hot," he murmured, and it turned me on even more, if that were even possible. "God, you're so fucking hot, so damn pretty." His voice was husky and deep. It moved over me like fingers stroking my body. He thrust his cock against my pussy, over and over again, back and forth. He was slow and easy, gentle almost, as if he were afraid to hurt me. And a part of me wanted him to, wanted him to just be rough and raw and uninhibited.

A small sigh, a long gasp left me.

Domink was long and thick, hot and hard.

He was mine.

It was all for me.

With his mouth at my neck and the feeling of his tongue running along my sensitive skin, all I could think about was the feel of him pressed to me, of his muscles against my softness, the fact that he was so masculine where I was feminine.

He groaned, but it sounded more like a wild animal. "Amelia, fuck, baby girl, once my cock is deep in your pussy, you'll know you're mine. You'll feel it. You ready?"

I nodded. I was so ready.

"Watch me," he whispered.

I shifted so I could look down the length of my

body. He gripped the base of his cock and started stroking himself from root to tip as he stared at me.

"Say my name, Amelia. Say it."

I swallowed. "Dominik."

He leaned in close and I held my breath, waiting to see what he'd do, what he'd say. "Want to know a secret?" I found myself nodding, not sure if I actually wanted to know. He smirked. "I don't feel bad at all that I kidnapped you, that I kept you in my room and made you think you were a prisoner." He thrust against me gently, letting me feel how hard he still was. "I don't feel one fucking ounce of regret."

And when Dom started touching me again, rubbing his fingers up and down the lips of my pussy, making me wet, saturated, all I could do was give him a soft moan as a response.

"That's it," he grumbled pleasurably. He slid his fingers into my body and I tense, the foreign feeling making me panic. "Shhh. I'll make this so damn good for you." He slid those digits in slowly, watching me the whole time as if gauging my reaction.

I closed my eyes and was about to beg him to claim my virginity, to push those thick inches into me until I couldn't breathe, couldn't think, until I was grasping for reality.

I could have gotten off from the way he used his thumb to rub circles on my clit as he gently probed me. I bit my lip, trying to reach that pinnacle, but a second later, he pulled his hand out from between my legs and pushed my thighs open wider so he could be fully wedged between them.

Dominik had his mouth by my neck, sucking and licking my flesh. There was this rhythmic feeling on the bed, this slight rocking. I realized why it was moving, why there was motion.

Dominik was dry-humping the mattress.

Oh my God. Why does that turn me on so much?

I lifted my arms and wrapped them around his neck, curled my nails into his flesh, and brought him closer to me. Then, I spread my legs impossibly wider and lifted up ever-so-slightly, wanting to feel some friction on my pussy.

He pulled back slightly. "God, your cunt feels like it's on fire against me." He leaned back even more, reached down and spread my pussy lips wide then just… stared at me.

For long seconds, he didn't move, didn't even seem to breathe as he looked between my thighs, at the area that was so obscenely open for him.

"I need to taste you, swallow you whole," he said to himself before he had his mouth on my pussy. His warm breath moved along my lips, the most sensitive part of me. He placed a hand on each side of my inner thighs, keeping me spread for him, the sting of my muscles being pulled from the act unable to take away the pleasure he gave me.

He worked his tongue around my clit and then moved it along my inner lips. The sound of him sucking at my flesh had me on the brink of getting off, but right when I was on the precipice of begging him to let me do just that, to add more pressure, he stilled.

Dammit.

He rose up, moved his tongue along my hipbone, over my navel, and stopped at my breasts. Then he dragged his tongue over one of my nipples, pulling a cry of ecstasy from me. I couldn't help but arch my back, pressed my breasts into his mouth, rocking my pussy against his cock that was like this steel pipe between my legs.

"Dom," I whispered his name.

Time seemed to stand still as we stared at each other. And then he pulled back enough he could look between my thighs once more. He reached down and took hold of his dick, stroking himself a few times before he placed the tip at my entrance and stilled.

"Tell me how much you want my dick, how much you want me deep inside your pussy."

I nodded. "Yes. I need it."

"I want to feel you from the inside."

His words were filthy but oh so good.

"I want to fuck you like an animal, Amelia." Dom started to push inside then, breaking through my virginity, my hymen. I instantly felt the stretch and burn from the size of his dick consume me. "I can't give you up. I'm addicted."

When he was balls-deep in me, he stopped. I clung to him like he was a life raft in the middle of the ocean. He only gave me a few seconds to adjust to his size before he started moving in and out, slowly at first, but with each passing second, he went faster, harder, and more thorough.

"So tight," he grunted. "So hot and wet. God, you're fucking soaked for me." He placed a hand on each of my inner thighs and continued to push into me, all the while staring at where he was buried.

"I should go slow, easy," he said, as if he spoke to himself, but it was only a second that passed before I saw something snap in him, saw it wash over his face.

He started to fuck me in long, hard strokes. Over and over, he pushed into me, the sounds of his cock slamming into my wet pussy making these erotic echoes off the walls.

Sweat covered my body, dotting his flesh too.

I reached out and grabbed onto his biceps, digging my nails into his skin, holding onto him, because I needed him closer.

My cry was slightly muffled as I came on his cock, my eyes closed from the pleasure.

Pumping into me fast and hard, Dom grabbed my hands and placed them over my head, keeping me in place as he dominated me, devoured me.

He hummed as he didn't let up on fucking me. "I can see on your face you like me taking control." He leaned in close and had his mouth right by my ear. "Is it because you've had to grow up too fast, take control of your life in every single way or you would've drowned?"

I closed my eyes and nodded, unable to actually say the words out loud.

"Say them then, Amelia. Tell me."

"God, yes," I whispered and came again, this orgasm smaller than the last but just as intense, as if it were a warm-up for a much bigger one.

My inner muscles clenched around his girth, as if my pussy needed him deeper.

Dom started pushing into me harder, faster, and I bit my lip and closed my eyes, the stretch and burn consuming me, the fact that Dom pushed into me and retreated over and over again taking all of my sanity.

"God. Fuck, Amelia." He slowed for a moment, easing through the tightness, and when he was fully seated inside me, he let out this hoarse noise.

I gripped the sheets, gasping for breath, the air in my lungs burning. His balls were pressed right against my ass, the heavy weight of them and the way he stretched me reminding me what we were doing.

"I wanted to go easy," he gritted out. "But I couldn't. I had to claim you."

I ground my hips against him, wanting him to move.

"Yes. Fuck, Amelia. *Yes*." He used long, powerful strokes to give me what I desired, his balls slapping against my flesh, his groans fueling me on. Reality was a distant memory. "Mine. Say it."

I stared at him with wide eyes. "I'm yours."

He growled. "Yeah, you fucking are." He slipped his hand behind my head and gripped a chunk of my hair, pulling my head back, baring my throat. God, I felt so vulnerable, so innocent. Another orgasm rose up in me, and all she wanted was to have it consume her. He tightened his hold on my hair a little harder and grunted as he slammed his dick fully into me.

"I wanted this to last, but fuck, Amelia. I can't baby." He started fucking me with more fervor and closed his eyes, his neck muscles straining, his body seeming bigger as blood rushed below the surface. "I can't stop. I'm going to come."

I opened my mouth and felt my eyes widen as I watched him orgasm for me, because of me. And then I came, just let go, feeling that tidal wave of ecstasy claim me.

He thrust into me once, twice, and on the third time, he stilled deep in my pussy and moaned. I felt the hot jets of his cum fill me, swore his dick hardened further, lengthened more.

Dom's orgasm seemed to go on forever, his body tight, sweat covering his form. It was long moments before I felt and saw Dom's big body relax.

I collapsed on the bed, my chest to the mattress, my breathing hard, frantic almost. I didn't think about anything but how good I felt, how incredible Dom made me feel.

He opened his eyes, staring down at me with almost wonder on his face. "You know what this means, Amelia?"

His expression was so intense, so severe. "This is how it'll always be for us." He pulled out of me and made a disappointed sound in the back of his throat. He brought me close and I relaxed against him, loving the heat that came from him, the way my body molded to his.

He was primal and intense, with this feral quality making me feel… secure, stable. I knew there was no going back.

When I really thought about it, I'd never really had my life as my own. I worked, went to school part-time before I took the semester off. I went home alone, watered a plant I could barely keep alive, and all I could do was picture a different life, a different world. My childhood had been tarnished and dark, just like Dom, and here was a new life staring me down with dark, stormy eyes.

"What do you want?" he whispered, moving strands of my damp hair away from my temple. "Tell me, Amelia." His voice was so soft, so gentle.

I thought about his question, about how maybe I could tell him the truth; maybe this was something I needed to accept, embrace.

"You," I said softly. I wanted to be with him, wanted to let myself just be free. I knew being with someone, with Dom, didn't mean all my troubles or my past, or anything like that, would fade away.

Broken bones didn't heal overnight.

Scars didn't just vanish.

He gently gripped my chin so I had to stare into his face, into his eyes.

"Mine, Amelia. You're all mine, forever."

And for the first time in my life since I'd met Richard, I actually felt like someone gave a shit about me irrevocably, no matter what, and until the end of time.

Chapter Eighteen

Dom

I held her, listening to the even sound of her breathing, letting it lull me to sleep. Although I wouldn't be able to close my eyes, didn't want to miss a moment, a second with her.

I kept thinking about Cullen near her, the threat, the fact that he could've taken her from me before I got there. It made my blood run cold. I held on to her a little tighter, pulled her closer to my body and buried my nose in her hair, inhaling deeply. That scent would be forever ingrained in me, in every single inch of my body, to the very nucleus of my cells, the very marrow in my bones.

"Is Richard okay?" she suddenly asked softly.

I knew who she was talking about, had scoped out that jewelry store before we'd robbed it, knew it as if I owned it myself. "Why wouldn't he be okay?"

She was silent for a second. "I saw him get hurt."

I shook my head. "We didn't touch him. He hurt himself by tripping. He's fine as far as I know. He's fine where we are concerned about it all."

She nodded slowly and I worried about her, about how she felt, about how she felt about me in all of this. I didn't want her to hate me because of this, didn't want any resentment, any animosity. I wanted her to… love me.

"I don't know anything about you," she finally whispered sleepily, her voice thick and drowsy.

It was sexy as hell.

"I'll tell you anything you want to know. All you have to do is ask."

She was silent for a moment, still. Then she shifted in my arms and I loosened my grip, allowing her to turn to face me. But then I had my arms right back around her waist, my fingers right at the little dip above her ass. God, I was getting hard again just having her close.

"Can you tell me about your life, your childhood?" She sounded a little hesitant about that, as if she were almost afraid to ask me.

I couldn't blame her for her reaction, because I'd taken her, she'd almost gotten killed twice, and I wasn't a good man. I was a bad guy, the villain in a movie or a book, the one no one really rooted for despite having the upbringing we did.

I started running the tips of my fingers along her arm, thinking about what to tell her, how to say it. I wouldn't lie to her. I wanted Amelia to know about me. This hadn't been about fucking her or keeping her like some kind of pet like Cullen said. This was real, the feelings I had for her strong and genuine… true.

"We didn't have the best upbringing, the greatest childhood, if I'm being honest." I stared into her green eyes, wanting to get lost in them, starting to feel like I was. In fact, I was getting lost in her, and her scent and feel, the way she touched me, looked at me… the way she resisted me but then gave in to me. "My father was a piece of shit, raised us to be the thieves we are. We didn't know love in our household." I was silent for a moment, thinking about the life we'd led, how Cullen had been the punching bag for our father.

"What about your mother?"

I shook my head slowly. "She stuck around for a while, but only long enough for Cullen and me to really remember her. After Frankie and Wilder were born, she left. The twins were only a year old at the time, so they don't remember anything about her."

I rolled onto my back and stared at the ceiling. I hadn't thought about any of this shit in ages. I tried not to. And even though it hurt to talk about it, dredging up this anger and rage I felt, the fact that I wanted to take it out on that bastard for all he put us through, I was glad I was telling Amelia.

"Cullen, being the oldest, got the brunt of our father's anger. He was a drunk and an addict, stealing to make ends meet, then using the majority of it to buy his booze and drugs. Cullen had more black-and-blue days than I want to remember." My chest ached as I remembered all the marks and cuts Cullen had endured, the pain my older brother had gone through to protect us.

"He wasn't always like this, you know." I looked over at Amelia and saw unshed tears in her eyes. Despite all the shit Cullen had thrown at her, she was feeling empathy for him.

"Dom." She whispered my name, and I felt my heart race.

"But life experience, my father, pain, and anger

made him who he was. Who he is. And he's been like this for as long as I can remember."

"But you said he wasn't always like this?" she asked softly, and I shook my head.

"No, he wasn't always like this. But that was when he was very young. He had to harden up really quick, had to become the person you've met. It was the only way he could survive. The only way he could protect us." I held her tighter. "But that's not an excuse for what he did to you, what he would have done because he thought it was the right call for the family."

She didn't say anything, but I could feel her emotion as easily as if it were my own. It was a strange connection, something I'd never experienced before. I wanted to hold on to it, to never let it go.

"I'm sorry. I know about shitty childhoods all too well." Her voice was soft but strong. There was no self-pity, and it was because she'd become hardened over time, like we all had when faced with adversity, degradation, and just being stuck in a shitty situation.

I wanted to know all about her, about what it was like for her growing up. I longed to be the person she talked to, confided in. But not now. The conversation we'd just exchanged had been enough. All I wanted to do was hold her, to let her know and feel that I was here, that I wasn't going anywhere. I leaned in and buried my nose at the crook of her neck, inhaling softly. She smelled like me and it was fucking incredible, had me hard and aching, wanting and desiring her all over again like I hadn't just been buried between her thighs.

"Why did you take me?" she asked almost too softly for me to hear.

I didn't move from the crook of her neck for long seconds, but then I pulled back and cupped her face with one of my hands, smoothing my thumb along her cheek, right below her eye. "I told you," I said just as quietly as when she asked me the question.

She shook her head slowly, staring into my eyes. I knew she wanted an answer, but I didn't actually have one to give. I couldn't explain it.

"This isn't something I do, kidnap women when I'm on a job, but I saw you and I felt something in me awaken, become alive." Those words hung between us, and I let her absorb them, to fully understand what I meant. And I knew she did. I didn't have to explain those words, my feelings. We were on the same wavelength.

I smoothed my hand down her neck, over her shoulder, and cupped her waist. She was so tiny compared to me. I leaned in and kissed her. "I can't let you go. I won't," I murmured against her mouth. Her breath was sweet and warm as it brushed against my lips. "You were mine from the moment I first saw you." I pulled back and stared into her eyes. "Say the words. Mean them." I said that harsher than I probably should have. "Tell me so I know you won't leave, so I know I won't have to chase you." I gave her one last, lingering kiss before pulling back again. "Because I will, Amelia. Chase you. Find you. I won't stop until you're mine forever. Tell me with no doubt in your mind that you know you're supposed to be here with me, that the stars lined up, the cards were in our favor, what-ever the fuck you want to call it, that you know with certainty that this was exactly the path we were both supposed to take."

She was silent for long moments, and I could see her mind working, saw the expression on her face. I didn't know what I expected, what I thought she'd say. Maybe I thought she'd tell me to fuck off or that I was crazy.

I was. For her.

But I held my breath as I waited for her to tell

me, to say the words or hit me, tell me this was a mistake, that she regretted being with me. And when she leaned in and was the one to kiss me, I knew she was mine. I knew with that one touch of her lips to mine, because she'd made the initiative; she'd been the one to reach for me.

"I'm crazy for saying this, feeling this, even thinking this," she whispered against my mouth. "But I feel like I am yours, and I don't want that to end, Dom. I don't want any of this to end."

It fucking wouldn't. Never. I was never letting Amelia go.

Chapter Nineteen

Amelia

One month later

I was always nervous when I met Richard for coffee. Even a month after the robbery and the situation with Dom, my heart raced as I expected Richard to tell me how stupid I was being and be judgmental.

But he never did.

"You're sure you're okay?" He always asked me that. Every week, probably expecting my answer to be different.

I nodded. "I'm fine. Are you?"

"Good. Really good actually."

I found myself smiling at his response.

He reached out and placed his hand over mine, which I still had curled around the ceramic of my mug.

"I can't say I'll ever understand this or accept why you are with him, Amelia. He's not a good man. Look at how he makes his living?" He shrugged and sighed. "But you're a smart girl. You're the smartest person I know."

I didn't know if I was all that, but hearing Richard say it made me feel happy, proud even.

"You were dealt a shitty hand in your childhood, but look at the woman you are now. Going to school, dealing with so much stuff on top of that. And despite all of the negative aspects that happened in your life, you still rose above and succeeded." He gave my hand another squeeze before pulling it back.

I missed the roughness of his fingers, the weathered feeling of his skin. It reminded a part of me of being home.

"And you know I will always be here for you, no matter what. I'm just a phone call away."

He gave me a smile and I gave him one in return, because I knew he'd always be there, because I knew he spoke the truth.

We continued to stay away from topics like

Dom or the jewelry store or the fact that Richard was moving away, that he was finally moving on with his life after his wife passed… after the jewelry store incidence. Our conversation was about the little things, the mundane things that had me laughing and smiling, that had contentment filling me. It was a conversation between two people who were just enjoying each other's company. It was a moment of two people who genuinely cared about each other, and I was glad he could understand where I was coming from, what I felt, and he accepted it.

He didn't try to change me, didn't try to sway my mind. He gave me his unspoken blessing, his understanding, and I knew he'd always be there. And that's exactly what I needed. That's exactly what anyone who had never had anything in their life needed.

But I did have something now. I had Dominik, and for the first time in my life, I actually felt like I wasn't alone.

I STOOD in front of Dominik's front door, the whole situation surreal and a little bit strange. This was the man who'd taken me, yet I'd driven away and come back. I was now about to go into his home like we shared it, like I lived here full-time.

It was crazy, but the good kind of crazy, the kind that had a person feeling like life had purpose, that there was excitement and anticipation to be had. I didn't know if anyone would ever understand me, but it didn't matter. Because I understood me. Dominik understood me.

That's all I cared about.

I brought myself back to the present and opened the door, stepping in. And in all honesty, the robbery and my time in his room all seemed like a distant memory now, like it happened to someone else so long ago now.

I shut the door behind me and heard commotion in the kitchen. I probably shouldn't have gone in there and interfered, but it was as if I was drawn to it, unable to stop myself from walking toward the noise.

I stopped before I got into the kitchen, standing right before the entryway, seeing all four brothers standing around the island. Cullen leaned against the stove with his arms crossed, the ball cap he wore pulled down low. He slowly lifted his eyes in my direction, and I felt a little shiver wash over me.

He didn't like me, didn't like my presence. He thought I was taking his brother away from him, his family. It didn't matter what anyone said on the contrary, because in the short time I'd known Cullen, I realized he was a solitary creature and went by his own rules.

"You can do whatever the fuck you want to do, Cullen, but it's bullshit and you know it." Dom was the one to speak, his voice clipped, terse. He was angry, and I knew this conversation was about me and the whole situation.

It didn't matter that it was obvious I wasn't going to turn anyone in, but I'd inserted myself into their lives, and it was clear Cullen was not used to that, didn't want to accept it.

"I have to agree with Dom," Frankie said. "I think this is just an excuse, because you're still pissed about not getting your way with the girl.

"Amelia," Dom snapped. "Not *the girl*. Amelia. Get it right next time."

Frankie held up his hands in surrender.

I couldn't help but smile at the sound of Dom defending me.

"If you want to leave, fine. But own up to why you're doing it," Wilder added.

Still, Cullen said nothing, just stared at me with those dead eyes.

A full minute passed.

"Let's make one thing clear," Cullen finally spoke, his arms still crossed over his chest, his baseball cap still pulled low. "I don't give a shit that you found a piece of ass, Dom, or that you're in love, or that you want to get married and have a houseful of kids." He shrugged and look at Dom. "I don't care if you've found your fairytale happily ever after."

I shivered at the tone of Cullen's voice.

"I need to get out of here, because we've been doing job after job. I'm going to the cabin to clear my head. When I know all of us are ready to focus, then we can start up again, yeah?" He phrased it like a question, but I knew it was anything but one. He looked at each of his brothers, and despite how hard Cullen was, I felt this emotion come from him.

I didn't know if the other guys recognized it, didn't know if they'd be able to see how hurt Cullen actually was. I understood to an extent. I screwed up their ecosystem, the way things had always been. He wasn't used to that. His only reaction was anger. He did what he had to do and made no apologies.

I didn't say anything, because I knew it would only makes things worse.

Cullen made a deep sound in the back of his throat and lowered his gaze to the ground, shaking his head. "I just need to get away, clear my mind. Without saying anything else or looking at anyone, he left the kitchen, walking past me, the breeze from his departure moving along my body and having goose bumps form along my arms.

Everything was silent for long moments after he shut the front door, and the sound of his vehicle leaving came through. Then there was a crack of thunder from the impending storm. I had felt it in the air, smelled the promise of rain as I stepped out of that coffee shop and came to Dom's.

I turned and looked back in the direction of the kitchen again. Frankie and Wilder were murmuring softly to each other and definitely annoyed, and Dom had his focus on me, an apologetic look on his face. I felt myself melt. It was clear he was worried about me, probably about how I felt after witnessing all that.

I didn't stop myself from walking over and wrapping my arms around his waist, putting my head on his chest, and just reveling in the fact that he was mine.

I didn't care that his brothers saw us or that I

felt their gaze strained right on us. I didn't care who saw the displays of affection we gave to each other.

"We'll hit you up later," Wilder said.

"Yeah, we'll leave you guys to it," Frankie added with amusement in his voice.

Then we were left alone. Dom had his arms wrapped around me as he kissed the top of my head.

"It's not you, baby," Dom murmured against the crown of my head. "Cullen's always been a lost soul. He'll leave at random for months at a time, going to the cabin we own a couple hours from here." He smoothed a hand over the back of my head. "Hell, we don't even know if he's alive when he leaves, because he won't call us, won't answer us when we reach out."

That broke a part of my heart.

"Aren't you worried about him just going off like that, not contacting anyone?"

I felt him inhale deeply and exhale just as hard. "No. This is how Cullen has always been. This is just who he is, has been ever since our father died and he didn't have to worry about the abuse or the fights breaking out between us."

I tightened my hands around him and closed my eyes. "Dom, I love you." I pulled back and looked up at him, my head tipped up in his direction. "I love you," I said those words softly, from the heart. This flicker of emotion passed across his face then he leaned down and placed his lips on mine, kissing me sweetly, hesitantly now.

"I love you too," he muttered against my mouth. "And I don't know what I did to deserve to have you in my life. God knows, I'm a fucking bastard, steal to survive, and have a shitty background, have done shit to stay alive that would have me going up in flames if I stepped into a church." He cupped the side of my face. "I'll show you for the rest of my life how much you mean to me, that I can be a good man to you, that I can be worthy of your love."

I cupped the side of his face then rose up on my toes and was the one to kiss him. I didn't know what to say in response. I needed to be worthy of his love too.

But instead of saying anything, I kissed him again and again and again, loving that two lost, broken souls could be whole if the stars aligned just right.

Chapter Twenty

Cullen

I should have slowed down, pulled over until the storm subsided, until I could calm down. I felt just as turbulent as the raging weather, as the hail slamming down against my windshield, as electrifying as the lightning cracking through the sky.

I felt like my life was spinning out of control once more, as if I were that little boy unable to stop his father form hitting him, unable to fully protect my brothers.

Dom found a woman he was happy with, and although she'd been this complication at first— something I knew I had to get rid of to save my brothers, our family—it was fucking clear she was his. He'd die for her.

He'd leave us for her.

I slammed my hand on the steering wheel, feeling like I had no control, like I'd never be able to have order once more. I lived my life protecting them, watching over them and cleaning up their messes. But they were grown now, living their own lives. Maybe I just needed to take a step back, reevaluate everything.

Find myself.

And so I had. I did.

I was going to go to the cabin, isolate myself there, make sure I was calm and levelheaded, knew my next step before I went back there. I wouldn't abandon them. I'd never leave my brothers. They were everything I had. The only thing I had.

The rain pelted the car and road, my tires barely catching the asphalt when I took a sharp turn.

I took another turn then straightened out the car, my tires squealing on the wet asphalt. I tightened my hold on the steering wheel, my emotions turbulent, consuming. I'd never been able to handle them when they did make an appearance, although I could hide them pretty fucking well.

I played that shit off like I was dead inside, and I supposed I was. But seeing Dom happy had a spark of something growing in me. His happiness made me fucking… happy.

Pretending I didn't have a care in the world, didn't give a shit about much of anything, was how I survived, how I kept everyone at arm's length. It's why I'd never been with a woman, had never claimed one as my own. I could've laughed at that fucking revelation.

Here I was, a thief, someone who'd gotten into plenty of fights, and had put plenty of men in the hospital. Hell, at one point, I even thought I'd killed someone. I wasn't a good man, never saw myself having a happily ever after. And if people thought I was fucking women and tossing them away, then I let them think that. What I wouldn't let them know, what I wouldn't admit, was the truth.

That I was a virgin, because I was afraid to get close to anybody, that I was afraid I'd hurt them, because I was so fucking messed up in the head. I'd given enough agony in my fucking life to last me an eternity. And so when I saw Dom happy, willing to give up anything and everything to be with Amelia, I didn't know how to react, how to feel. And something in me had just snapped. Something in me had risen up violently and I wanted to extinguish the threat.

And that was wrong of me. It was wrong of me to try and take something away from my brother that he held so dear, to take away that happiness he deserved tenfold.

I took another turn, my car skidding to the side before I was able to right it. The rain was coming down even harder, even more violent.

I should have turned the car around, should have apologized to my brothers for all the shit I put them through, not just because of the situation but in general. I knew I was a hardass, a bastard and asshole at the best of times. I was horrible at showing how I cared for them. The way I showed them was beating the shit out of somebody who'd talked bad about them, and picking up extra work when we were on a job—hell, giving them more of my cut and not telling them about it.

They were my baby brothers, and I'd do anything for them, but I couldn't keep them under my wing forever.

I took another turn, should've slowed down. In fact, I should've just pulled off to the side of the road and waited the storm out. But my mind was racing, my thoughts cloudy. And I took the next turn way too fucking fast, my car hydroplaning, everything moving in slow motion. I tried to get the steering wheel corrected, tried to straighten out the car. But everything was spinning, the vehicle turning around and around before slamming into a tree and rolling into a ditch.

And right before my head smacked against the steering wheel, right as I knew what was going to happen, I thought about how I should've fucking turned around.

Epilogue

Amelia

Several months later

I looked down at the blueprints of the Wilson Estate then glanced up and stared at Dom. "Are you sure you're ready?" I didn't miss the tremor of nerves that came through in my voice.

Dom leaned against the far wall, looking down at the blueprints, even though I knew he couldn't see them clearly enough to decree what the layout was. "We got this, babe," he said in a deep, masculine voice then lifted his gaze to look into my eyes.

I swallowed, my throat tight, dry. I was nervous, worried for him, Frankie, and Wilder. I always got worried when they went on a job. This wasn't about them getting caught and thrown into prison. No, this was me imagining the worst-possible scenario, where they were shot and killed, taken from me.

Over the last half a year, I'd become part of this family, realized what I'd been missing in my life wasn't a family unit per se, but *Dom's* family unit. The twins were like brothers to me, Frankie and Wilder clearly the more easygoing out of all four of them, the two who genuinely enjoyed life and probably partied too hard. And as much as I wished I could say the same thing about Cullen, the truth was, he'd left months ago and hadn't come back.

To me, that screamed worry and uncertainty, but Dom assured me that he occasionally did this. He needed to be alone. He needed to work out his life, and when he was ready, he'd come back and they'd be there.

A solitary creature didn't need comfort or love. It just needed to survive. And that was Cullen.

I looked back down at the blueprints and started worrying my bottom lip. Over the last six months, I'd moved in with Dom, stopped working at the jewelry store, and was all-in where this "business" was concerned. I was insane—that was a given for how this entire situation played out, but then again, when something felt right and perfect, you just jumped in with both feet.

And that's what I had done and hadn't looked back, hadn't regretted a single moment of this journey.

"You talk to Richard?" Dom's voice was right behind me, deep and thick, washing over me and nearly having my eyes close in pleasure.

"Earlier this week." I thought about all that happened in the last few months. Richard had sold the jewelry store—not because of the robbery or anything like that, but because it had been time for him to move on to greener pastures, so to speak.

I told Dom how Richard had decided to enjoy his golden years, to try to make peace with the fact that he didn't have his wife anymore. He needed to do something to find pleasure in living again.

He'd officially retired, moved to the country, and was just enjoying fishing every day and sitting by a fire at night, drinking whiskey. I talked to him weekly, something I wanted to do, and not because I had to. He was my family.

And despite the fact that he might not agree with everything that happened, my choice to stay with Dom, the fact he had no love for the man who

I was in love with, I knew he cared about me and knew I could make my own decisions.

Maybe he didn't think it was smart or realistic to be with a man who robbed people for a living and who had kidnapped me, and I guess it wasn't, if I really thought about it. But that didn't change the fact that this was how I wanted my life to be, who I wanted to be with.

I was a firm believer that everything happened for a reason.

I felt Dom slide his hands around my waist, curling his fingers against my hips. He pulled me back slowly, gently, the hard length of his erection prodding my back, my eyes closing as I made a sound of pleasure. I was instantly wet for him, primed, and all it took was the sound of his deep voice, the touch of his fingers along my arm.

There was nothing more I wanted in this moment than the man who was with me right now. Well, nothing more than living this life that had been thrown in my path.

I felt his mouth by the shell of my ear, his warm breath tickling the sensitive skin. I rested my head back on his chest, could hear and feel the steady beat of his heart. He was calm and collected, as he always was, but that didn't mean he was relaxed.

Not when I felt his hard cock digging against the small of my back, showing me exactly what he wanted, how much he wanted me.

We said nothing as he moved his hand over my belly, down to the waistband of my jeans, and expertly flipped the button undone with his two fingers. Then he slid the zipper down and slipped his hand under my panties. My mouth parted and a silent sound of pleasure left me when I felt his palm cup my pussy, his finger teasing my hole.

My inner muscles clenched, and I didn't stop myself from spreading my thighs a little wider, giving him better access. The deep rumble that left him was satisfied, pleased.

"You're a dirty little girl, aren't you?" He asked the question, but I could tell he already knew the answer. He ran the tip of his tongue over my earlobe. "So wet and greedy for my cock." Dom gently bit on my ear, sending a shockwave of tingles throughout my entire body.

Yeah, I didn't want him to stop, but right now, I wanted his cock in my mouth, wanted to feel it hit the back of my throat, wanted to swallow all of his cum.

Before he could stop me, give me his dominance, and fuck me right here on the table, I turned around in his arms, his hand being pulled from my pants. He held up those fingers glistening with my pussy cream and brought them to his mouth to suck them clean. He stared right in my eyes the entire time. And then he hummed in pleasure, as if I tasted so fucking good.

My knees nearly buckled. Now I was the one unbuttoning his jeans and pulling the zipper down. He lifted a dark eyebrow and smirked, just the corner of his mouth tilting up. But he didn't stop me, didn't say anything as an arrogant expression covered his face.

I pulled his jeans down to free his cock then looked down at the massive length. The tip was already dotted with pre-cum.

"Well, well." I glanced up to him from under my lashes. "Look who's ready for me." I was the one to smirk now, and I saw his smile fade as this intense expression covered his face.

His chest started rising a little bit faster, a little bit harder when I gripped the base of his shaft and started stroking him from root to tip, my palm sliding over his length fluidly, easily. He felt like hot velvet over steel.

I smoothed my palm over the tip of his dick and watched the way his jaw clenched, the muscles under his cheeks flexing. He was wet for me, his pre-cum a constant presence now that I was touching him. I used that seed as lubrication as I brought my palm down his length, back and forth. And then I held my hand up and showed him my palm, clear fluid smeared along it. Now I was the one to run my tongue over my hand, licking away that salty proof of how worked up he was for me. And the groan he gave me was a victory in my corner.

I didn't waste another second as I dropped to my knees and stared at his dick. He was so big, as thick as my wrist, so long I knew I wouldn't be able to fit it fully in my mouth from experience. But I'd sure as hell try to get as much as I could, not just because I knew he loved that, but because I fucking enjoyed it as well.

With one hand, I cupped his balls, the heavy weight substantial in my palm. And then I opened my mouth as wide as I could go, feeling my jaw pop a little as I leaned in and engulfed the head first then slowly slid down his length. He had his hand in my hair, his fingers tangled in the strands almost painfully as he held my face to his crotch.

And then I started bobbing up and down, blowing him in the way I knew he liked, letting the crown of his dick hit the back of my throat until I gagged, until my eyes watered. He pulled my head back ever so slightly, his dick still in my mouth, my lips suctioned around the tip. I had my gaze trained right on his eyes. He lifted his other hand and smoothed away one of the tears that started falling out of the corner of my eye.

"You look so fucking pretty with my cock in your mouth and those tears sliding down your cheeks." The way he murmured those words was as if he were talking to himself, as if he hadn't meant to say them out loud or meant for me to hear them. "Now suck my cock until you make me come, Amelia. Know that you're the only who will ever be able to do that."

My pussy clenched at his words, at his meaning and the truth in them.

"Suck it harder, Amelia, faster." His voice was starting to get harsher, gruffer with his rising pleasure.

I lifted my hands and gripped his thick thighs, my nails digging into them, my head moving up and down seemingly on its own. Saliva pooled in my mouth as I took as much as I could. I slid one hand to the base of his cock and started stroking his dick with what my mouth couldn't reach, feeling his entire body tense. He was going to come for me and I was going to swallow it all. I was greedy for it, hungry. And then he groaned, an animalistic sound that had me reaching between my thighs.

I slipped my fingers under the waistband of my jeans and panties, stroking my clit furiously, needing to get off, wanting to orgasm right along with him.

"That's it, baby," he groaned roughly. "Stroke that pretty little pussy of yours as you suck on my cock like a good girl." He had both hands in my hair now, pulling at the strands, thrusting his hips forward as he pushed my head down. He was mouth fucking me in the dominant, possessive way he did with everything in his life… with me.

I closed my eyes just as I peaked, just as my orgasm washed over me. I hummed around his shaft, moving my tongue along his dick, right along the thick vein that ran on the underside.

"God. Fuck yeah." And then he came, trying to push all of his inches into my mouth until the crown of his dick was lodged in my throat, as he pumped his seed into me, making me drink it all, not letting any drop slip free.

Tears ran down my cheeks, and I held back my gag reflex, swallowing every ounce of his semen, wanting more. And when he was finally spent and had pulled back, only then did I allow myself to suck in a great lungful of air. I still had a hand between my legs, my inner muscles clenching, my clit tingling and throbbing. I stared up at him with my mouth parted, feeling the wetness on my face, knowing my eyes were still watering.

He reached out and ran his thumb along my bottom lip, gathering a drop of cum, pushing it back into my mouth. "Lick it all off," he demanded, and I greedily did what he said.

God, he tasted so good, so male and potent. So mine.

He helped me to stand and immediately embraced me, wrapping his hands around my waist, pulling me in close. Dom slammed his mouth down on my lips, thrusting his tongue in and out. I wanted to beg him to fuck me, plead with him to give me what I desperately wanted. And that was his big cock taking ownership of my cunt.

He kissed me like he was desperate for me, dying for me. I felt consumed and claimed, grasping for him, gasping for air. He pulled away and we both sucked in air, our chests rising and falling. My head felt dizzy, my knees weak. I could've crumpled to the floor if he hadn't been holding on to me. And then he slowly smirked, slid his hands down to my waist, and before I knew what was happening, he had my jeans and panties off.

He lifted me easily, setting my ass down on the table. He had his hands on my knees and spread my legs wide, stepped between them, and grabbed hold of his cock.

"You ready for me, baby girl?"

I licked my lips and nodded. I didn't think I could've spoken in that moment.

He leaned in close, his warm breath teasing me, exciting me. "I love you," he said softly, gruffly.

I closed my eyes and rested my head on his shoulder, inhaling his scent, letting it go deep into my body.

"I've only ever loved you. I will only ever love you, Amelia." He started kissing my neck, moving his lips up to my jaw and then to my mouth. He made love to my lips and tongue, electricity moving through me, content mixing with my excitement and arousal.

"I love you too," I whispered, murmuring against his mouth. I reached between our bodies and grabbed his cock, placing it at the entrance of my body. He pulled away and cupped my face with both hands, staring into my eyes.

"You're the best thing that has ever happened to

me, that will ever happen to me." His voice was hard and genuine, his expression matching. "I would die for you, Amelia. I would kill for you."

I felt the truth in his words. I loved this man more than anything else, couldn't even picture my life without him anymore. We were one and the same, these once empty, hollow vessels that had never had the chance of being filled. But then we'd found a purpose with each other.

Soulmates.

"I love you, Dominik." And then he thrust into me, filling up not only my body, but my heart, my life, my very soul.

And who would have imagined I'd feel those things for a professional fucking thief, like he'd said plenty of times.

And God was he right. About everything. About us.

The End

HE ONLY WANTS
HER

STALK
HER

USA TODAY BESTSELLING AUTHOR
JENIKA SNOW

STALK HER

By Jenika Snow

www.JenikaSnow.com

Jenika_Snow@Yahoo.com

Copyright © September 2019 by Jenika Snow

First ebook publication © September 2019 Jenika Snow

Photographer: Reggie Deanching

Cover Model: Ryan Lee Harmon

Cover design by: Lori Jackson

Editor: Kasi Alexander

Content Editor: Kayla Robichaux

As president of The Devil's Right Hand MC, I could get whatever I wanted.

Drugs, women, money, but most of all power.

And it's the latter I was most interested in, most focused on acquiring. Because without that, you're nothing. And in the town of Copperhead, Colorado, I had no problem making people bend to my will.

I ran my club with an iron fist, and what we did wasn't exactly legal, but then again the kind of money we wanted, you didn't get by following the rules.

So back-alley deals, corrupt situations, blackmail, and just being a downright bastard… that's what the MC was known for.

That's what I was known for. Because fear got you what you wanted.

But then *she* came into my life—this sweet, fresh, and pretty young thing working at one of the bars the MC owned. I should've stayed away, should've kept my distance, because she was a liability and a distraction I sure as hell didn't need.

Yet all it took was that one encounter, that one moment for her to cross my path, and I was completely obsessed with her.

I found myself doing anything and everything to get information on her, to find out who she was, where she lived... why she was so far away from home.

So I followed.

But her life wasn't as innocent and vulnerable as she wanted people to think. She had secrets. She had a past. One she was running from.

But I wasn't into a fairytale life or ending. That was never in the cards for me.

Because when it came to her, I knew I'd do anything to make her mine.

Chapter One

Butcher

"Either fucking fold or quit pulling our dicks," I said as I glared at Right Hand, a fellow patch who'd gotten his nickname because he'd nearly lost his damn right hand after he'd been caught fucking his stepbrother's ex-girlfriend. Even though she'd been an ex, apparently said stepbrother still had a hard-on for her and went after Right Hand with a butcher knife. He nearly took the fucking hand right off like he was trimming meat for Sunday dinner.

Besides, the nickname fit with him being a member of the MC and all. Now, Right Hand had a gnarly scar around his wrist, and a sweet-ass biker name to go along with it. Guess things worked out the way they were supposed to.

And you'd think Right Hand would have learned from that mistake, that a life lesson like that would have knocked some sense into his crazy ass. But nope. Fucker was still sleeping with said step-brother's ex on occasion all these years later.

Must have been some damn good pussy to risk having a motherfucker come after you with a butcher knife again and go for another part of the body.

"I'm not pulling anyone's dick but my own," Right Hand said and grinned, flashing a silver cap on one of his side teeth.

"I know you don't got anything, asshole. So fold already, so I can go home and crash. I'm fucking beat."

He exhaled and threw down his cards, face-up. The other three guys followed suit.

"Too fucking rich for my broke-ass blood," Boss said.

"I think you bastards like pulling each other's dicks with this pissing contest." Nitro was the next one to speak.

And then there was Scorpion, a patch who I even wondered if he spoke English, given the fact that most of his communication was in grunts and nods.

"That's what I thought," I said and tossed mine down, showing a pair of twos.

"What the hell? You don't even have shit." Right Hand's face was turning a nice shade of red as his anger rose to the surface.

"Had a shit hand… yet here I am, taking all you motherfuckers' money." I grinned and reached for the center of the table, pulling the cash toward me.

"Fuck," Right Hand muttered. "I'm getting drunk and getting laid. Fuck this shit."

The rest of the guys started talking shit.

"Go lick your wounds, you fucking crybabies." I flipped them off and reached for my beer, finishing it off before I left. I had a long-ass day tomorrow, and it wasn't even doing fun shit, just paperwork and legal bullshit for our legit businesses.

We might be outlaws, but hell, we weren't stupid. Having on-the-books businesses kept us on the up-and-up. It made sure we looked like law-abiding citizens, even if we sure as hell weren't.

I was nearly done with my beer—just set down

the bottle on the scarred table—when movement out of the corner of my eye had me turning and looking in the other direction.

She walked out of the back room, carrying a tray. She was tiny as she leaned against the bar and waited as Richie made up her drinks. Her jeans were tight, too tight, because they showed off her slender frame and the way her ass popped out.

It looked juicy... like a fucking peach.

Her cropped top wasn't obscene, didn't show skin, but it was tight enough I could see how small she was all around.

Fuck, I bet my hands would wrap fully around her waist.

She was young, too fucking young to be working in a place like this.

She was too fucking young for me to be looking at her the way I was, thinking about the things I was.

Her long blonde hair was pulled into a ponytail, and the first thing that came to mind was how I wanted those strands wrapped around my hand as I took her from behind while I yanked her head back and bared her throat.

I tracked her movements through the bar as she set down the orders at different tables. Her cheeks were pink as if she were blushing. Fuck, she was innocent-looking. I didn't stop myself from lowering my gaze to her chest. Her tits were small, maybe not even a handful. But they looked perfect. The little nipples were poking through the material, making my dick instantly hard and press against the zipper of my jeans.

The men who frequented this bar were lowdown criminals, outlaws like myself. They took what they wanted and asked questions after the fact. And a girl like her sure as fuck shouldn't be in a place like this.

I didn't like it.

I called Richie over, the manager of our establishment. He came over with a towel slung over his shoulder, a worried expression on his face. He wasn't like us, like the MC. In fact, he'd been the original owner of the bar before we took over, before we gave him an ultimatum, no choice but to go into business with us.

That's what kind of bastards we were.

"What's up, Butcher?" Richie asked. The older man might not be a criminal like myself, but he sure as fuck wasn't some law-abiding citizen. That's why it made it easy to give him the ultimatum to sell us his bar while we still allowed him to run it.

What could he do? Refuse us and end up in the back-alley dumpster?

Besides, he was good at selling underage customers, also good at selling pussy in the back of the shop during and after business hours.

"Who's the new girl? She barely looks old enough to buy a pack of cigarettes, let alone be serving alcohol."

Richie looked over to where the young blonde was and then glanced back at me. "That's Poppy. New girl. She's been here about a week. Just turned nineteen, I think." The look he gave me was a little bit hesitant. It was the look of a man who thought I said something shady. He knew me well, but fuck, I wasn't some kind of a fucking maniac. "Should I have asked before hiring her?" he asked genuinely.

I shrugged. "I don't give a fuck who you hire, Richie." I looked back at Poppy. "You selling her ass in the back like the others?" He better fucking say he wasn't or I'd break his kneecaps. That thought and certainty filled me so strongly it shocked the hell out of me.

"No." He shook his head adamantly. "She's not a whore. She just slings drinks and collects a paycheck every other week."

I grunted in response. "Poppy," I said under my breath, instantly liking how it rolled off my tongue.

I could still feel Richie looking at me, but I didn't give a fuck. He wasn't my concern. Now, Poppy... Poppy was definitely my concern.

Now Available: https://amzn.to/2ODAAHS

About the Author

Find Jenika at:

www.JenikaSnow.com
Jenika_Snow@yahoo.com

Made in the USA
Lexington, KY
29 November 2019